TOMMY TILLER
AND HIS DOG RUDDER

JOHN MARTIN

This book is the second edition. Some changes in form and content are present.

This is a work of fiction. Names, characters, and incidents are products of the author's imagination. Every effort is made however for places and terms to be accurate. All geographic locations have been personally sailed by the author.

Cover design by Charles MacEachern

Printed in the United States of America.

ISBN: 1452891656
ISBN-13: 9781452891651

To JEMKEM
For teaching me the joy of storytelling

ONE

It was just one of those days you always remember. I was in the backyard, sitting below the kitchen window, trying to get my bike chain back in place. It had come off for about the tenth time and I was ready to toss the stupid thing into the street. I had moved the rear wheel as far back as it could go, but the dumb chain kept coming off. Truth was, however, I really didn't care about the bike. I was just working on it to keep myself out of the house. I had placed it as close to the window as possible for strategic reasons: having a project just outside the kitchen window allowed me to know when my dad got home. I needed to know (1) that he was home, and (2) what my mom was going to say to him. And it was preferable to get this information from a safe distance.

Normally I would pay no attention, but I was in big trouble that afternoon. I had been dreading my father's arrival but I knew that time would come. When it finally did, I wanted to be positioned to get a preview of what I was in for, and at least give myself enough time to make a run for it if I had to.

It was pretty easy to tell when my dad got home. First I would hear the garage door open, then, like always, my dad would head straight for the kitchen and I would hear the familiar sound of the refrigerator door opening and my mom saying, "Don't drink the milk out of the container, Mr. Neanderthal." Next came the sound of a glass being placed on the counter and the milk pouring from the container into the glass.

My senses were fine-tuned. I could even hear him drink the entire twelve-ounce glass in a series of big gulps. I pictured my mom standing there, giving him just enough time to finish his milk before filling him in on the day's events. As I heard the glass touch the counter for the second time that afternoon, I waited for my mom to speak, but was surprised to hear my dad's voice first, "Honey, I've had enough. My patience is at an end and I think I'm ready to make the move."

There was a moment of silence. "Uh-oh, this can't be good," I thought. Obviously my mother must have called him at work. She replied, "Are you talking about what I think you're talking about?"

"Seriously, honey, if you're ready as well, then let's make it happen. We can take Tommy out of school at the end of the term and start our new life by June."

Their conversation had my undivided attention. I knew I was in trouble because I had been sent home from school three hours early that afternoon after a little lunchtime fight. My mom was not happy about being called out of work to fetch her delinquent son.

The whole thing was a bum deal because it wasn't my fault. I was just hanging out with Sally Zimmerman when big-shot Ricky Spitz came over and told me to get away from his girlfriend. Sally seemed surprised, but not nearly as surprised as I was when I heard her say, "You're not my boyfriend; Tommy is."

My first thought was to check if there was another Tommy around besides me. Sally wasn't just some girl: she was the prettiest girl in the school, maybe in the world, and here she was standing right next to me declaring me—Tommy Tiller—her boyfriend.

With this news, Ricky was more than a little irritated. He got in my face and pushed me to the ground, all the while telling me to hit the road.

So there I was, sitting on my butt in the dirt on the school playground. At first, I wasn't sure what to do. Other kids were gathering around. Sally was holding her hand over her mouth, a look of shock on her face. The truth was that I was the one in shock. Suddenly, out of nowhere, I was the new boyfriend of the most popular girl in sixth grade. Me, Tommy Tiller, a guy who had never actually had a girlfriend before.

Even sitting on my butt I knew I had been elevated from chump to prince. This left me with a tough question: "Now what should you do, Prince?"

As any newly appointed knight in shining armor would do, I got up and pushed Ricky Spitz back. Next thing I knew, we were rolling around on the ground going at it until a couple of teachers picked us up and marched us down to the principal's office.

It was a long walk through the hallways. I had only been going to this school for one year and this was my second trip to the principal's office. The school was a lot bigger than my old school, and I figured that the walk I was on must be what it's like in prison as you march past all the closed doors on your way to see the warden.

My mom was called and advised that I had been released from school for the rest of the day. Actually, for the rest of the week. Odd system, I thought. My punishment was *not* going to school. Makes a guy want to get into more trouble. If there had been no such thing as parents, I would have strived to stay on the suspended list.

Reality kicked in when I heard the sure footfalls of my mom marching toward the office in her high heels. Her steps actually sounded different when I was in trouble.

It was a long ride home in the backseat of the car. Mom wouldn't even let me sit in the front seat. The worst part was that she didn't say one word to me for the entire drive. I guess I knew that most of the discussion was going to be handled by my dad when he got home from work. To make things worse, he had been at work since the previous night, so he was already going to be cranky. As an orthopedic trauma surgeon, he was often called into the hospital in the middle of the night. It was just my luck that this was one of those times.

So there I was, listening to my dad say he was ready to "make the move." I got more and more nervous. It sounded as if he was talking about getting rid of me! The whole thing about "having had enough" and the stuff about taking me out of school seemed a bit over the top. I thought surely my mom would speak in defense of keeping me. Instead, her excitement level went up, and in her excited "Honey, I love you" tone, she said, "Are you kidding? I have been waiting a long time for this day, and I am more than ready."

At that point, I knew I was done for and figured an orphanage was probably the next place I'd call home. To make the whole thing worse, even though I couldn't see through the window, I was pretty sure they were kissing. They were actually happy about this!

They finally left the kitchen. I stayed outside with my broken bike, bewildered. I wasn't sure what to do. I tried to process what I had just heard. It was the first time I had ever been suspended. I had gotten detention a couple of times—well, seven times, to be exact—but had never been suspended before. Of course, most of the detentions weren't really my fault.

I stayed out of the house as long as I could, surprised that my dad had not come out to hunt me down even though it was getting dark. Finally, I had no choice but to sneak in the back door. Our house was fairly big, but there was only one set of stairs that led to the second floor and my room. My plan was simple. I would slowly and ever-so-quietly creep through the kitchen and grab a box of Pop-Tarts on the way for my in-room dinner. Once through the kitchen, I would cross along the back wall of the living room and head toward the stairs. It seemed possible with all of my family—my sister Caroline included— sitting with their backs toward me. The plan was in motion, and as I made my way, I could see them making marks on a world atlas.

"Holy smokes," I wondered. "How far away are they sending me?"

Passing within about two feet of them, I made my move to the stairs. No one noticed—not even a glance was cast in my direction.

"Boy, this is bad," I thought. "Really bad."

My dad had his arm around my little sister, the princess that she was, showing her various places on the map. Oh, what a day for her. Not only did she always believe she was the only child who mattered, now she would actually get to *be* the only child.

I made it to my room undetected, quietly closed the door, and sat at my computer. I knew I had to think of something. Maybe an Internet post of "New parents needed for cool eleven-year-old kid, ASAP." Another option was to run away, set my own destiny, be my own man. The thing was, at eleven and a half, I suspected there would be issues. I mean, I didn't really have any money. I didn't have a car, and I didn't even know how to drive. Of course, there would be the food issue, and where would I sleep?

It became more and more clear that there would be no easy way out. The worst-case scenario would be an orphanage, but I figured, really, how bad could that be? I even found myself wondering if orphanages have baseball teams.

Then I remembered that I did have one option. A few months earlier, my dad had had a long talk with me about how I was getting older. He told me there would likely be a time when I would find myself in a bad situation. A situation that I might have allowed myself to get into perhaps with friends or at a party, where things such as alcohol or drugs might be present. He had given me a piece of paper about the size of a business card with the words "Get out of jail free" printed on it. He explained it as a one-time—and one-time only—use card. If I put myself in a bad situation, I could call him, get picked up, and then pass him the card and no discussion would be needed.

The problem was, however, I was pretty sure I would need that card some day in the future and did not want to use it just two months after getting it. And I didn't know if it would apply in this case, with the school having already given out my sentence.

The important thing was to have a plan and avoid panic. If I just laid low for a while, I might blend into the background. If I made no sound and stayed kind of invisible for a few days, they would forget about me. After all, they had Caroline, the "perfect daughter." I didn't talk that much anyway and I was out of the house most of the time, so sure, they might forget about me long enough to forget that I was in trouble. Even if it wasn't the best plan, it was still a plan.

Unfortunately, before I could even turn off my light, there was a knock on my door followed by my dad's voice. "Tommy, I want to talk to you."

I sat in silence. I thought perhaps he would just go away if he thought I was asleep. Chances would have been better had it been later than seven o'clock.

No luck. The door opened and my dad came in, looking serious. I decided to take the offensive and go right at him with, "You don't understand. It wasn't my fault."

Imagine my confusion when he replied, "What wasn't your fault?"

This was a tough position. How does one answer that? I was confused. Did he not know? Had my mother left out that little detail about me getting suspended? At that point, I figured if he didn't bring it up, then the only thing for me to do was shut up.

The whole thing was happening very fast. I decided to change gears and replied, "Sorry, Dad. What's on your mind?"

"Tommy, your mother and I have made a decision—a life change, if you will. We have decided to sell the house, buy a boat, and sail around the world."

It was that matter-of-fact.

I was trying to pay attention to what he was saying, but that last statement was hard. I was more than confused. I was totally lost.

I asked him to repeat what he had said, but when he did, it came out the same. After hearing it again, we both just sat there for a while. He seemed to be waiting for my mouth to close.

When I came out of my state of shock, I asked the obvious question: "Is Caroline going with you?"

He replied, "Of course she is. Do you think we would leave her behind?"

He started going on and on about the plan to explore the world, all the while not mentioning me.

Finally, I had to interrupt him and ask, "Uh, Dad, am I going?"

He stopped babbling and said, "Of course you are. We are all going. The whole family."

This created another moment of confusion for me as I could not help but wonder if being included was a good thing or not. His plan of buying a boat and sailing around the world made the orphanage idea sound pretty good.

He went on. "It's a simple process. We find a nice, well-built sailboat, prepare her for crossing oceans, do homeschooling, and head out to explore the wonders of the world."

The whole conversation seemed so unreal that I didn't know how to react. Did this mean no Sally Zimmerman, no friends, no baseball, no anything but my parents and Caroline on a little boat forever?

Perhaps it was the stunned look on my face that prompted my dad to fetch the globe. "You see, son, we will start here. We'll have a cutting-of-the-lines party at the Chicago Yacht Club, then we'll head out into the Great Lakes, hitting all but Lake Superior. Then we'll head out through the St. Lawrence Seaway into the Atlantic Ocean. From there, the world."

"What in the heck is a 'cutting-of-the-lines' party?" I asked.

"Son, it symbolizes the cutting of the lines that tether us to the dock and land," my dad answered. "It means we are released from the bonds of normal life and are off to the unknown."

"This is just great," I thought to myself. "The unknown." Either my dad had flipped or I was having a nightmare. How could a day go from getting into a little trouble at school to leaving everything in normal life to sail to the "unknown"? It was too much to wrap my head around.

My mind was in overload. I found myself unsure. Was I in trouble? It seemed for now that I wasn't. That was good news! On the other hand, it seemed as if my dad had lost his marbles. That was bad news! I mean, come on, was he serious? Live on a sailboat? He must have forgotten that both he and my mom had jobs.

And then there was the concept of homeschooling. It made no sense. Granted my mom was a college professor, but only in physics. Who would teach all the other subjects? There was also the issue of Caroline. She went to a small private school. My parents seemed to think she was some kind of brainiac and actually moved us to Chicago just so she could go to some dumb "gifted" school. When we lived in Owosso, Michigan, I was the top dog on the baseball field, so moving to Chicago had been a pretty big sacrifice on my part. I went from the best on the team to working my way up to the starting lineup over half the season. I also gave up all my friends, had to sell my dirt bike since there was no place to ride it in Chicago, and lost my weekend job at the Ice Cream Shack. Both my parents changed job locations and even bought a new house, all just so the princess could go to some special school. To decide to up and leave everything and go sailing seemed crazy!

I had to admit, though, that my dad sure looked excited. The last time I saw him that excited was when I was heading off to summer camp for a week. He had that same look of anticipation and joy on his face as I prepared to leave. My guess was that his excitement would fade when reality returned, just as it had when I came home from camp. I figured this was the same sort of thing—a short-lived fantasy of my father's that would soon diminish.

I assumed that in the end, my mom wouldn't really go for it. I knew she liked her job at the university and she seemed to be something of a star there. When we lived in Michigan, she had to commute one hour each way to the University of Michigan, but now in Chicago, she just took the subway six stops and was a block from her office. Overall, she had a good gig here.

I did, however, remember stories of my mom as a rock climber and some of the adventures she'd had in college. She even did ice climbing in Alaska. She loved adventure, so I started to wonder if she would be of any help.

My dad went on for another half hour, babbling about the plan. When he finally stood and moved toward the door, I felt a great relief that he was leaving my room. Just when I thought the worst was over, he opened the door partway, turned, and and said, "By the way, tomorrow when your mom gets you up at seven, there will be a list of three days' worth of chores for you on the kitchen table. I will inspect each one when I get home from work and cross off only those done right. If I'm not happy, the list will grow indefinitely. You're going to really miss school." Then he walked out and closed the door.

I wasn't sure how to digest what had just happened. The sailing around the world idea was so crazy, I figured there was no way it would really happen. As for the future, that didn't matter. I could handle the punishment. Sally Zimmerman was my girlfriend, I wasn't heading to an orphanage, and life would likely be back to normal in a few days. At least, that's what I thought.

TWO

Things were very different around our house for the next four months. Each day when my dad came home from work, he sat at the computer and researched boat stuff. All conversations between he and my mom were now about boats and junk you put on them.

I didn't care. Summer vacation was only a couple of months away. By then, my dad, with the help of his golf clubs, would forget about his crazy sailing idea. I had seen him change his mind plenty of times. I was pretty sure he would change his mind about this, too.

With each passing week, new packages and boxes arrived in the mail. Each was anxiously opened by my dad. Each held a new piece of sailboat junk. Several books came, mostly titled *Cruising Guide,* about different places on the globe. Then there were the maps, or charts, as my dad called them. I'd never seen anyone so excited to look at maps!

One package caught my attention: a big box from UPS. It held a red duffel bag filled with what looked like miles of rope. My dad lifted it out of the box as if it weighed a hundred pounds, which I later learned it did. He unzipped the duffel to inspect the contents.

13

He stretched the rope across the full length of our yard and back again—twice. At the far end of the rope hung a thing that looked like a parachute. My dad explained that it was a drogue. "You see, son, in extreme weather, when the waves build up to twenty feet and larger, we can drag this chute three hundred feet behind the boat to slow us down," he added.

It didn't even occur to me just how big a twenty-foot wave was, but I was curious as to why we would want to go slower. I had to ask. "Why would you want to go slower?"

He couldn't wait to tell me. "Well, Tommy, in really big seas, the boat can surf down the face of the wave and pick up a lot of speed. So much speed that at the bottom of the wave, the nose can go under and the boat can be turned upside down. It's called broaching."

My mom, who was standing next to us, seemed unconcerned.

"Mom, are you listening? Did you just hear what he just said? The boat can get turned upside down!"

To my shock, she simply said, "Honey, that's why we have a drogue."

I was at a total loss for words. It was official: they had both gone totally mad. Part of me still believed that time would cure them, but with summer quickly approaching, they seemed on course for being committed to a mental hospital. What made no sense is that they had it all. My dad was a surgeon, my mom was a professor, I was a really cool son, and Caroline—well, I don't know about her, but she completed the whole American dream thing of a house in the suburbs with a yard and two kids. To leave it all behind to sail to the "unknown"? It was clear that they had both cracked.

The undeniable reality of my situation came just after Easter. My dad took us on a road trip to a town called Racine, about an hour north of Chicago. It was there that the confirmation of my parents' mental collapse became clear. As our car approached the water of Lake Michigan, I could see the marina. It looked deserted. The boat slips were empty and several boats sat on the land covered with blue plastic. It was pretty easy to find a parking spot, since we were the only car in the lot. My parents and Caroline couldn't get out of the car fast enough. They looked excited as we walked around the marina office to the docks.

We strolled down a long, cold dock. The ice had barely gone from the winter. There was one boat in the water at the far end, and we were heading straight toward it. At the end of the dock, we all stopped, and my parents just stood there for the longest time looking at the thing as if it were their newborn baby.

The two of them pointed and mumbled to one another. I wondered what could possibly be so interesting. It was just a boat, for crying out loud. A boat floating alone in an empty marina, as if abandoned by some other couple that had come to their senses. For a moment, I thought that after they had their look, we would turn around and head back to the car and out for some fast food. Unfortunately, my dad stepped onto the boat and said, "Come on, guys, step aboard."

Caroline leaped over; my dad had to catch her from bounding right into the water on the other side. My mom was all smiles as she took my dad's hand and stepped down to the deck. She turned to look at me and said, "Come on, Tommy. Come see your new home."

"New home?" I remember thinking. They had to be kidding. This was not home. This was a floating tent without the tent. Something you might camp out in for a weekend at the most. A home? No way. It was still dirty from sitting through the winter, and there was nothing about it that would suggest it had any potential to be a home for anything other than some adventurous mice.

My dad unlocked the padlock on what looked like a door, which allowed him to pull out three boards that closed off the cabin from the outside. We walked down about six steps into the cabin. It was actually larger than I thought it would be but still pretty small overall. My mom opened the shades, my dad flipped some switches that allowed lights to be turned on, and Caroline was running around to every spot on the boat like a puppy fresh out of her cage. I felt more like the dog who had just been put in his cage.

My dad went straight to the engine compartment while my mom started going through cabinets in the kitchen. Turns out that kitchens on boats are not actually called kitchens, they're called galleys, but in reality they're just small kitchens.

There was a separate cabin with a bed in the back of the boat that was a pretty good size, a smaller room in the front with a bed shaped like a triangle, and then two small bunk beds on one side. There were two toilets, one in the back and one up front, but from what I could see, there was no obvious way to flush them. It took me all of two minutes to see all I needed to see and I was ready to go. Unfortunately, I was alone in that feeling.

I was already getting bored and still could not believe that any of this was happening. I figured I would find a television and watch a show or two while the rest of them did whatever it was they were doing.

I searched everywhere, but there was not a single television—zip, none, nada. Not even one of those little LCD types you can put in a corner. After extensive searching, I asked my mom.

"Well, of course there's no TV, Tommy," she said. "How would you connect the cable a thousand miles from land?" She laughed, I didn't. It seemed we were supposed to live in the dark ages, like my parents had when they were kids.

With nothing else to do, I kept exploring. It only took about five minutes to discover everything from one end of the boat to the other, but it wasn't clear where I would sleep. I assumed I wouldn't get the larger room in the back, so I asked my dad, "Where's my room?"

Rather proud and excited, he answered, "Come with me, son. I will give you the grand tour."

We moved toward the room in the front, but before reaching it, he said, "Here you go, Tommy. This is where you will sleep—the port side sea birth."

"The what?" I asked.

"The port side sea birth, just to your left."

I turned and looked into this little—and I mean little—room with two small beds, one above the other. I was really starting to think this was all just a bad dream, so to test reality I asked, "Where does Caroline sleep?"

He pointed forward to the much larger room with the triangle bed.

"Of course," I thought to myself. "The princess gets the big room while I live in a closet." Now I knew it wasn't a dream, but rather the normal flow of things for Tommy Tiller.

As the day went on, things only got worse. After sorting out who slept where, my dad went on to tell me, "Now, you know you and your sister will have to share the same head."

What in the heck was that supposed to mean? Share the same head? How do you share a head? And even if we could, whose head would we share?

Of course, Caroline would want to use hers, since she believed her head was filled with a lot more information than mine. I would like to argue that, but it did drive me crazy that she could do my homework better and faster at barely ten years old. I know this because it cost me two dollars a project. I didn't get that, either, because I knew I was a lot smarter.

Anyway, as my dad was explaining this sharing thing, he was pointing to a small bathroom. It turned out that the bathroom on a boat is called a head. None of this made any sense. Like the left side of the boat is called the port side instead of just the left side and the right side is called starboard, the bathroom is a head. Head? I mean, really, how stupid could anything be? The list of new names for things that otherwise had normal names went on and on. I gave up even pretending to listen.

The boat seemed okay for fishing or something, but my crazy parents were saying we were not only going to live on it full time, but we would also be crossing the oceans. The oceans! The oceans were huge on the globe, certainly too big to get across in a little boat.

Had they not heard of airplanes, hotels, and rental cars? The stuff normal people use to see new places? I was sure that Christopher Columbus would have chosen a Boeing 747 over his beat-up sailboat, had they been invented yet.

I could feel myself getting pretty down as the hours passed, so I put my brain back into thinking about more important things, like how tomorrow's baseball game would go. When I finally made the starting lineup, I was batting eighth and playing second base. Now I was batting cleanup and playing short. I figured that at this rate, I would be playing for the Cubs by the time I was twenty, and if by then my parents were still sailing to nowhere, I would simply send them postcards.

Finally, after what seemed like a week, they were done looking around the boat and ready to head home. I was first to make for the stairs. I noticed going up the steps that they were all curved at the edges, almost U-shaped. "Why are the steps curved?" I asked my dad.

He replied, "They're curved so that when we're sailing and the boat is heeled over, it makes it easier to get up and down. And by the way, that is the companionway, not the stairs."

Sure, that made sense. Take a simple word like "steps" and change it to "companionway," like everything else on a boat you can't call by a normal name. It has to be something that makes no sense, just like the idea of living on one.

It seemed like a long car ride home, but before I knew it, all the nutty boat stuff was over and I was back in my real house, with real bedrooms, several TVs, a kitchen you can call a kitchen, and where the only heads were the ones attached to our necks!

That night at dinner, I couldn't resist asking, "So, Dad, really, tell me the truth. You can't be serious about living on that boat. Tell me what's really going on."

He acted insulted. "Son, this is one of the finest boats in the world. She is made by Moody, one of the most respected boat builders in the world. Built in Plymouth, England, and shipped here to Lake Michigan. Built to cross oceans with style and all the comforts of home."

"All the comforts of home?" I thought. Whom did he think he was kidding? It didn't have *any* comforts of home.

This wasn't the first time I'd disagreed with my dad. I wanted to continue the argument, but he reminded me that I still had six years, three days, and some hours before I could legally be in charge of being right.

As time passed, I tried not to let all the sailing stuff get to me. I focused on more important things like Sally Zimmerman and baseball. School had actually become a place I wanted to be, a place where there was no talk of living on a boat and where most of the people were sane.

I rarely saw Caroline. She went to a private school near the university where my mom worked. It wasn't really clear why she was in a private school. Every morning, she had to leave at seven o'clock with my mom—way too early for me. She also did a lot of schoolwork with my mom when they got home. She seemed pretty smart for a little kid, so I didn't under-stand why she needed so much extra attention.

Caroline was particularly good in arithmetic. In fact, I was paying her two bucks a week to do my math homework. I never actually watched her do it, but it didn't seem to take her very long. I should have rene-gotiated a better rate. Although I did wonder why she didn't go to school with me, I didn't wonder enough to ask. It didn't matter anyway, as we were getting close to the end of the school year.

At home, my parents continued to talk every day about boats and places to go on them. It was as if there was nothing else going on in the world. Finally, a day arrived when I was sure I wouldn't have to hear about it—my birthday, a kind of holiday, if you will. Personally, I'd say that my birthday is the best day of the year. Better than Christmas given that I am the only one who gets presents and I don't have to give any. I also get to be free of chores for the entire day. Even my sister, Caroline, has to take a back seat.

This was my day. I ruled! My mom made a big, yellow, double-layered cake with white frosting and twelve perfectly arranged candles.

When the big moment came to blow out the can-dles and make a wish, I knew exactly what to wish for. It was a no-brainer. Out went all the candles with a single blow and a clear wish: Someone fix my parents!

Although I believed nothing would get to me that day, my mood started to dwindle with the first pres-ent. It felt strange—a bit flexible and oddly shaped. I tore off the paper.

"Surprise!" my mother shouted. "It's your own PFD."

"PFD?" I replied. What in the world is a PFD?

My sister, who gleefully piped in, interrupted my mother in her excitement to explain, "Personal floatation device, dummy."

"A what?" I asked.

"Your own life jacket, Tommy," my mom clarified.

I wasn't sure what made me angrier: getting something so lame for a present or that my ten-year-old sister knew what a PFD was.

Then came the next present. "Great," I thought. "Smaller, solid feel—it must be some cool add-on for my game box." Off came the wrapping paper and—wow—a little light on a little yellow plastic box.

I didn't have to ask. Caroline once again jumped in. "Personal strobe light for your PFD. Helps us find you at night after you fall into the ocean."

"This can't really be happening," I thought. It was my birthday, for crying out loud, and I was being tortured.

There was still hope, however. One gift remained and it was sure to be a real present.

Small, flexible, and about the size of something to hold a bunch of cash! "Yep, this is it! Cold hard cash." I could spend cash wherever and on whatever I wanted.

I unwrapped it and to my unfortunate shock it was nothing but a little blue book with my picture inside and a cover that read "Passport, United States of America."

They must be kidding. No real presents, no cash, nothing!

This was one of my best birthdays ever. *Not.* It was crystal clear that my life, the life of one Tommy Tiller, was officially over.

THREE

June 4. I had been out of school for summer break all of one day, and rather than hanging around with friends, I was sitting alone on the dock outside the Chicago Yacht Club. My challenged parents and Caroline were inside having the party of a lifetime celebrating our big "D-day"—our planned departure for the next day. Good-bye to real life, to baseball, to girls, and to TV, and probably good-bye to people under the age of forty. For me, that big party marked the end of civilization—or at least civilized life.

It really bothered me that my parents didn't even consider how I might feel about the whole idea of living on a boat. They never even asked me if I wanted to go. They just assumed I would share their excitement, when in fact I shared none of it. I had made a few good friends in my first year in Chicago, batted just over three hundred for the first time in any season, and was finally feeling like I fit in. Now I was being forced into another move, only this time a lot worse.

I looked across the harbor from the yacht club and could see our boat tied to the dock. The back—er, sorry—the "stern" flashed me with the name my dad had proudly painted: *Imagine.*

Even though I still kept thinking this wasn't real, that boat was out there, almost daring me to come aboard. Daring me to take that step into nowhere. It had blue sides, as if it was going to try and hide in the ocean so even the ocean wouldn't know we were there. And again, that name stared back at me: *Imagine.* "How about imagine this…" I thought. "We stay home and be normal people!"

After about an hour, I decided it was time to go inside the club, not that there was anything for me to do in there. It wasn't as though there would be any other kids or anything, but I was hungry and that's where the food was. I was suffering enough and I figured I shouldn't add starvation to my misery.

Entering the Chicago Yacht Club, I felt way out of place. It was pretty much all adults, with the ladies all dressed up and the men gathered in groups talking about who knows what. No kids, no fun—just adults laughing for reasons unknown to me, drinking their champagne.

As I strolled through the back door and looked across the ballroom, I could see Caroline holding a glass of lemonade as if she'd just stepped down from the bar with her favorite martini. She was wearing her best dress and talking with grown-ups as if she was one of them. Did I mention that she was ten? The strange thing was that they talked to her as though she really was one of them. I just looked at them and thought, "Something in the world—no, the universe—had gone wrong. Like, really wrong."

People came up to me to said things like "Congratulations" or "You are so lucky." I kept wondering if they really knew my father's plan. I tried to ignore them and made my way to the food table. Standing behind the table was a guy serving with a big white hat that stuck up about two feet over his head. I looked at the first pan of food and asked the guy what it was.

"This, my boy, is escargot."

"Escar-what?"

He replied, "Snails, lad. Would you like some?"

"Ah, no thanks," I said. "But how about the one next to it over there?"

"Yes, good choice, young man. That is caviar."

Well, it looked harmless, but I had to ask, "What's caviar?"

"Fish eggs, kid."

Fish eggs? That couldn't be true, so I asked again.

"Yes, you bet, and the best fish eggs you will ever eat."

"How about the best fish eggs I would never eat!" I thought.

Frustrated, I looked to the next pan and was afraid to ask. As I got closer, it appeared I wouldn't have to. Sure enough, it was octopus. I wondered at that moment if it was okay for a guy to cry now that he was twelve.

It seemed I was going to have to add starvation to my list of sufferings after all. The idea of an orphanage was sounding better and better. In fact, I wondered if could go online and apply. I walked away from the food table with my head hanging low and sat in the corner at a small table by myself. The chef guy must have seen my pain, because about ten minutes later, he came over with a silver tray covered by a round silver top. He removed the cover to reveal a huge half-pound cheeseburger and spiced fries. I looked up at him in a way that he knew he was my new best friend.

The party finally ended at about nine, and the four of us walked around the club to the docks and made out way onto our new "home." I went straight to my bunk, closed my eyes, and hoped that in the morning it would all have been just a bad dream.

Very early the next morning, my dad shook me awake, saying, "Come on, Tommy, get up. You're with me on first watch."

I didn't bother to ask what "first watch" meant. After all, this was still just part of the dream, wasn't it? But with another shake from my dad and his voice close to my ear saying, "Get up. Time to shove off," I had to face the unfortunate reality of my life.

It was cold at five in the morning. I really did not want to leave my bunk, but it was clear that there was no getting out of my dad's orders. Before I could even get my pants on, I heard the engine start up. That terrible sound signaled the fact it was all really happening. I went to the bathroom—oh, in this world, the "head"—but found myself almost afraid to go. Although my dad had showed me how to flush, I hadn't paid much attention. This was not your person-friendly toilet. There was the regular—well, kind of regular—bowl and seat. Next to the seat was a T-shaped handle for pumping up and down. There was also a dial with only two positions, one labeled "inflow" and the other "outflow." I couldn't remember what position the dial was supposed to be in before pumping.

My dad had been pretty specific. Seemed it was important to get it right. I really had to go, but figured I could hold it for a little while. I didn't know how long I could hold it, but given my dilemma, I was about to find out. I went up the companionway into the cockpit—another odd term. I always thought cockpits were those cool places where pilots sat in jet fighters. A place I planned to sit someday.

It was strange looking around. My dad was busy getting last-minute things taken care of. The skyline to the north was peaked with all the tall buildings of downtown Chicago. To the east, the sky was deep red, and to the west it was still very black. I don't think I had ever seen the sun come up before. I had to admit, it was kind of cool. It was easy knowing where north, east, and west were as I was standing in front of a big compass by the steering wheel.

My dad jumped back into the cockpit from the deck and said, "Tommy, ready the starboard bow line."

Even upon my first order, I knew it was not going to be pretty. My dad had spent hours with Caroline and me going over boat terms. Why would I bother paying attention at that time? Back then, I still believed the whole idea was the result of some bad food my dad had eaten and would never actually happen. Apparently, he was still eating the same bad food.

My dad could see I was confused.

"Tommy," he said, "go to the front of the boat and un-cleat the line on your right and then hold fast."

Why, oh, why, are people unable to just speak regular English on a boat?

At that point, I had the part about going forward to my right, but was confused about the un-cleat and hold fast thing.

As I got to the front, I could see a rope wrapped around a silver horn-looking thing. It didn't take a rocket scientist to figure out that that was the cleat. Obviously un-cleating was taking the rope off, but what about the "holding fast"? I figured I'd just grab it fast.

The wind was blowing into my face as I looked to the right. My dad had already untied the ropes on the left "port" side.

I did what I was told. I grabbed the rope "fast" and took it off the cleat, and then let it go.

"Tommy," my dad yelled, "why did you let go of the line? I told you to hold fast."

Turns out "hold fast" means "don't let go."

The wind was now blowing the front or "bow" of our boat onto another boat next to us.

It seemed my dad wanted me to hold the line on the windy side until the boat started backing up. Lucky for me, our boat has small propellers underwater facing sideways on the bow. These little babies are called bow thrusters, and with the touch of a switch in the cockpit, the bow was pushed in line as we backed out, no damage done. Tommy was spared.

As he backed the boat out of the dock, my dad turned the wheel all the way one way, then moved a throttle handle on the right side of the wheel to the forward position.

The boat slowed and started to move forward. My dad turned the wheel all the way in the opposite direction and we were now heading out of the harbor.

As we passed a long line of piled-up rocks that formed a break wall, I could see the open water of Lake Michigan. We had to pass around to the right of the first break wall and then turn "to port" to head out between two more outer break walls.

This formed what they called the outer harbor in Chicago. My dad said you had to be careful here because there were often a lot of boats moving in and out of the opening to Lake Michigan.

As my dad stood at the wheel, he looked over at me and said, "Tommy, come take the helm."

After my usual empty stare, he clarified, "The wheel, Tommy."

Is he kidding? Me, drive?

I stepped around the big wheel and looked over the bow of the boat. I had to stand on the part you normally sit on so I could see. Then the craziest thing yet happened. My dad said, "Hold her steady, Tommy. Stay to the starboard side as you leave the harbor and then turn north-northeast."

He got up, walked forward, and disappeared into the cabin. There I was, alone, driving this thirty-six-thousand-pound ship heading to the open sea. In command and captain of all hands on deck. Okay, so I was just captain of me, but still I was captain. As I approached the narrowing between the two final break walls, it seemed to get smaller and smaller. I wasn't sure we would fit.

"Of course we will," I said to myself. This was how all boats enter and leave the harbor.

I was okay as long as I stayed to the starboard side. I even remembered that starboard was to the right. I was fine. It didn't take long, however, before my first moment of panic. A big boat was approaching from the opposite direction. My heart was pounding about a thousand times a second. Do I call for my dad? What if I mess this up?

With my hands almost melted to the wheel, I stayed on course. The "big" boat turned out to be a little fishing boat, but it still looked big in that narrow opening. My eyes stayed glued to the opening as I watched it approach to my left. Then they passed to my port side and waved as they went by. I felt cool. After all, I was captain.

In the main part of the lake, there was nothing but water as far as the eye could see. Nothing but open Lake Michigan.

My dad had said to steer north-northeast. Although I was a bit unsure of that instruction, the big compass was right in front of me. Clear as could be, there were markings all around it: N, NNE, E, SSE, S SSW, W, NNW. Even I could figure that out. I just turned the boat to the port until the little centerline was lined up with the mark "NNE." I felt pretty cool.

A bit later, my father popped up with a cup of coffee for him and a hot chocolate for me. "Good heading, Tommy."

I felt smart. As much as I wanted to stay in command, I had to ask my father to take over. I had determined exactly how long I could hold it. I needed the head now—like, right now. My dad took the helm and I bolted toward the companionway. As I started down, he said, "Don't forget to put the lever in the outflow position when you pump."

"I know, Dad," I replied, thankful for the hint.

After a successful pee and toilet operation, I was right back in the cockpit.

"Do you need me to take over?" I asked.

"Sure," my dad replied. "Come on over and let's plot our course on the computer."

I jumped right back into my captain position and took the helm. "What computer?" I asked.

"This one," my dad said, and removed a plastic cover from a box sitting above the compass.

"This, Tommy, is a chart plotter. It's a computer that holds copies of all the charts we need and shows us exactly where we are on the chart. We can plot a course and simply follow the route."

He spent about twenty minutes going over the basic functions and buttons. It was not all that different from some video games I had played. One thing cool on this boat was the autopilot. My dad had explained it to me weeks earlier when I was paying no attention, but now I could see just how cool it was. The autopilot was a gadget that steered the boat for you. You could just put in the compass heading you wanted and push a button and it took over. Very cool.

On the chart plotter, my dad started entering "waypoints." Each waypoint is a place in the lake you want the boat to go. You can place waypoints so that the boat follows a course that goes around things like islands and lighthouses. You just enter the points that define the route and presto, the autopilot will follow it. Of course, I didn't need the autopilot as I could steer the boat just fine on my own.

FOUR

On our first day, we planned to sail to Beaver Island, up toward the top of Lake Michigan. According to my dad and the chart plotter, it was two hundred and seventy miles away. When I asked my dad how long it would take to get there, he said, "Well, Tommy, look at the boat speed indicator. You can see we are going six and a half knots. The island is two hundred and seventy nautical miles away. So you tell me how long it will take."

Then I heard the familiar, irritating voice of Caroline from the bottom of the companionway. "About forty-one and a half hours."

I just looked at my dad and said, "I knew that."

It was only about six-thirty in the morning and Caroline was up, dressed, and ready to go. She was supposed to be on watch with my dad from eight to ten, or, in our new boat lingo, from 0800 to 1000, but there she was, up and ready one and a half hours early.

I often asked myself what was wrong with that girl.

She came into the cockpit as if she had been doing it her whole life wearing a thick sweater, jeans, and her new little deck shoes. She had a smile on her face and a glass of juice in her hand and was ready to sail to the ends of the Earth. I was impressed by how relaxed she was—no worries, no fear, just excitement and energy. She looked at me in position at the helm and said, "You know we have an autopilot."

Again I wondered, "How does she know this stuff?"

As much as I liked steering, I got a bit bored after a couple of hours and asked my dad to take over. He took over, all right—he reached over and pushed one button: the autopilot! Yep, I could see how important my steering skills were—*not.*

By eight, my mom was up making breakfast in the galley. With the wind blowing pretty good, the boat was leaning over a fair amount. This, I learned, was called "heeled over." Maybe they call it that because to stay in your seat, you have to dig your heels in not to fall out.

Heeling makes it hard to walk around. As the boat leans one way, you have to lean the other way when you walk, so you feel like you are always walking at an angle. Not the most natural way to move around. My mom had the interesting task of making food while standing crooked.

We sailed all day in nice weather. The sun was out and the wind kept us moving. "This is lame," I said to my mom. "After seven straight hours, we've only gone fifty miles."

Caroline piped up and said, "Well, Tommy, that's actually about fifty-seven regular miles."

"What are you talking about?" I asked.

I got that typical Caroline look of "you dummy" as she went on to say, "The boat and chart plotter use nautical miles, not regular or statute miles."

"So?" I replied. "A mile is a mile. Doesn't matter if you're on water or land."

She looked at me like she was talking to a little kid. "That's true only if you are using the same kind of mile. The plotter is using nautical miles, and each one of those equals 1.15 statute miles, the type of mile we normally use on land. So if you think about when we are driving in the car, that fifty nautical miles you are seeing on the plotter is really fifty-seven road miles."

It bothered me sometimes how matter-of-fact Caroline was about such things. It wasn't even that she was trying to be a know-it-all. The stuff just flowed out of her mouth. I looked at my mom and she just shrugged her shoulders. I looked back at Caroline and wondered, "Who is this creep and where does she get her information?"

Timing, however, couldn't have been better. My mom and sister were heading back into the cabin to start putting together school lesson plans, and my dad was just resurfacing after a short nap. "Tommy, how far have we gone?" he asked.

After a quick glance at the chart plotter, I said, "Fifty nautical miles, or, by my calculation, about fifty-seven statute miles."

My dad's jaw dropped. "Very good, Tommy. Bonus points for you. Sometimes I think I underestimate you."

"You can say that again, buster," I replied.

The rest of the day was uneventful, but given that I had been forced to get up so early, I went to bed at about eight-thirty that first night at sea. I was out like a light and slept until around midnight, when my dad rudely woke me up.

"Come on, Tommy, watch time."

Now all it takes to be on watch is to look out for other boats and stuff, so why does it take two of us? I pleaded, "Come on, Dad, can't you just do it?"

That was followed with the prompt response, "You have five minutes. Get your butt moving."

Just when I was starting to think this was going to be fun, that disturbing thing called reality struck again. I wasn't even sure it was legal for a parent to force their kid up from sleep to take watch. I knew I should have researched my rights and that whole child-labor rules thing you hear about. Until I could figure out how to mutiny, I was stuck having to get dressed again and head out into the darkness.

Sitting in the cockpit in the dead of a moonless night was eerie. The chart plotter display glowed softly. Dim lights glowed just over the companionway from the instrument panel, showing boat speed, wind speed, wind direction, and how deep the water was under the boat. Looking out, I saw nothing. I could hear water running under the boat and wind moving through the rigging, but couldn't really see anything outside the cockpit.

"So this is exciting," I said to myself. "You just sit and stare into space you can't see."

After about an hour of being on watch and looking at nothing, I finally noticed some lights forward of us off the starboard bow. I couldn't tell how far away they were, but I pointed to it and said to my dad, "Land ho, off the starboard bow." It was kind of fun saying that. I felt like I was on a big pirate ship.

My dad said, "No, son, that's a ship."

I looked again and replied, "Sorry, dad, I hate to tell you, but that's land."

He seemed to chuckle. "Okay, Tommy, just keep an eye on it so we don't hit the 'land.'"

I did just that. I stayed focused and on task. Problem was, the land seemed to be moving from the starboard side across to the port side. After about twenty minutes, it disappeared way off to port. Not long after, my dad asked, "How we doing on that land?"

"No problem, I just steered around it."

Again he seemed amused. "Good job." I was glad Caroline wasn't sitting there with me. In my head, I even called myself "dummy."

The cockpit was actually pretty comfortable. It was near the center of the boat, so this kind of sailboat was called a "center cockpit." There were long seats that started at the companionway and ran the whole length of the cockpit, then curved around behind the helm. The backs were high enough so that you could sit and rest your back against them. At two in the morning, I found myself sound asleep on the starboard side. Because the wind was coming from the port side, the boat heeled toward starboard. Lying on the "downwind" side kept me leaned up against the backrest—all and all a pretty comfortable spot.

The sound of my dad moving around the cockpit woke me up. He was changing how the sails were set up. Hard to explain, but the sails on this boat didn't really go up and down. They went in and out. They were called "roller furling sails." I was hoping my dad thought I was awake the whole time and just resting, since I was technically on watch. I suspect he was so focused on changing the sail setup he didn't even notice.

We had two sails in front of the mast. The one farthest forward, the larger of the two, was called the jib. The one just behind it was smaller and called a staysail. Then there was the big one straight up from the cockpit just behind the mast called the mainsail.

My dad seemed to be in a hurry as he wrapped a rope around a metal drum called a winch, which was used to help pull on the rope.

"Tommy, this line I put around the winch is called the furling line. It will wrap up the jib so it's no longer out." He showed me a button just to the right of the winch and said, "When I tell you, just push the button and keep pushing until I say stop."

My dad looked at the chart plotter and called me over. "Look here, you see?" He pointed at the screen.

The last time I looked, it only showed the marine chart. Now it was covered with a lot of yellow and red.

"Looks different," I said.

"Sure does, Tommy. That's because we are now looking at the radar display on the same screen. All that yellow and red is rain—and a lot of it. There's a storm coming down on us and it's only eight miles away."

My first thought was to ask if that was nautical miles or statute, but my dad wasn't looking playful.

"So, Tommy," he said, "time to shorten sail."

This meant to bring in some sail so there was less exposed to the wind. He flipped on the autopilot and positioned me at the electric winch button. He then went to a larger winch on the starboard side of the cockpit where a large rope was holding the jib sail in tight.

"Tommy, when I release this line, I want you to push the button and start bringing in the jib."

As my dad slowly let line off his winch, I started bringing line into mine by pushing the button. The jib got smaller and smaller until the whole thing was wound up around the forestay. Then we tackled the main sail in a similar fashion, and in the end, only about half of the main sail and the smaller forward sail were out, with the jib rolled up completely.

Normally, if we didn't leave the cockpit, my dad didn't make us wear life jackets, but at night, we always had to wear one. My dad connected a safety line with clip-on hooks, one end to my lifejacket, the other end to a ring on the floor He said it was called a lanyard and would help keep me on the boat. He then did the same to himself. This was followed by closing the companionway door and positioning himself at the helm, autopilot off.

"Get ready," he said.

"Get ready for what?" I asked.

"The squall will hit us in about three to four minutes. It's only a mile away."

"Squall?" I asked. "What's a squall?"

"Hang on, because you're about to find out."

The wind came out of nowhere and hit us like a hurricane. The needle on the instrument that showed wind speed shot up to over fifty-two knots, which, according to Caroline's math, worked out to about sixty miles per hour! The boat heeled so hard that I was sure it was going to tip over. The mast almost touched the water. I would have been tossed out of the cockpit if it wasn't for the lanyard tethering me.

The wind blew so hard that the boat was almost completely on its side. My dad seemed to be fighting with the helm as he turned the wheel hard. Then the rain came. Not normal rain, but something I could not have even imagined. It was like we were already under water. It came so hard it felt like it would take the skin off my face.

My dad was three feet away from me and screamed something, but as loud as he was yelling, I couldn't hear a word over the noise of the wind. So much water was coming in the boat that surely we were going to sink. The cockpit was flooded up to my knees. Had the companionway been left open, the cabin would have been just as flooded. The boat would almost be level again and then another gust would lay it back on its side. I couldn't figure out why we hadn't tipped all the way over yet. Somehow, the boat managed to keep coming back up each time it got knocked down.

I kept looking back at my dad. It was very odd; he didn't seem scared at all. In fact, he was almost enjoying it. I, on the other hand, was not so much into it as I was sure this was the last day of my rather short life. Even though I was connected to the boat by the tether, I was still holding on with all I had. Even in the darkness, I could see the white foam on the top of the giant waves before they smashed onto the boat, each time forcing us over onto our side. I was so scared that I had to remind myself to breathe. It helped that the lanyard was keeping me onboard, but I imagined that same tether holding me to the boat as it sank five hundred feet to the bottom of Lake Michigan.

What seemed like hours ended up being about thirty-five minutes of sheer terror. Finally, just as fast as the storm hit, it was gone. No wind at all, not a puff. The sails went limp and the boat barely moved, and we were level again. The water in the cockpit quickly drained out the back while I checked to see if I'd peed my pants.

My dad unclipped us both and opened the companionway door. I backed down the stairs, flipped on a cabin light, and could not believe my eyes. Everything was everywhere. Books were on the floor, plates from the galley were up near my bed, it was an overall wreck. My mom was quick to come out of her cabin.

"You guys okay?" she asked.

"Sure, no problem, Mom," I said.

At about the same moment, we all realized that Caroline was nowhere to be seen. How beat up would she be after being tossed back and forth in her cabin? I raced forward with both of my parents behind me and opened the door. There she was, eyes closed, back up against the starboard hull, looking kind of peaceful. No movement. I couldn't even tell if she was breathing.

The boat knockdowns had been violent, but surely she was okay. I approached her still body and shook her a couple of times, but nothing happened. I started to turn toward my parents for help when Caroline said, "What do you want, dummy?"

I was never so glad not to like her. The girl had slept through the whole thing! Seemed impossible. I mean it, she was *not* right.

Throughout the night, several more squalls hit us, though none were as strong as the first. It started to become routine. We made the sails smaller for each squall, and then brought them back out for the calms. I felt like I was getting the hang of changing the sail setup. I also started to feel calmer, even in control. It had become clear that we—and the boat—

could take it. By daybreak, things looked good again. The sun came up, the waves weren't too big, and the boat was moving along at a steady seven knots.

By about noon on our third day, we put into our first port, a place called Beaver Island, Michigan. It was nice getting off the boat, but it was also kind of strange. Caroline and I sat in a little ice cream shop called Daddy Frank's. It was only a short walk from the boat. We were both looking forward to a chili dog, fries, and some ice cream. The odd thing was that I still felt like I was moving, even though I was sitting still. I looked at my sister and could swear she was rocking a bit as well. "Caroline, why are you rocking?" I asked.

She replied, "I'm not, the floor is."

I started to feel sick. We decided to take the food to eat as we walked back to the boat. When we got back on the boat, the feeling that things were moving stopped. I stopped feeling sick, too. I can't explain it, but it felt steadier on the boat than it did on solid land.

We were docked about fifty yards from the ferry dock. When the ferry came in at two pm, it was packed with people and cars. As I watched the people disembark, I noticed a girl about my age with her parents. Once off the boat, they started walking toward the marina where we were docked. Later I learned they were looking for friends who had come over on their motorboat from the mainland.

As they got closer, I could see that the girl was really cute. She had long curly brown hair with blue eyes and looked as if she belonged in a magazine. I waved and said hello. The mom replied in kind, and asked if we'd seen a powerboat called *Endless*. I told them we hadn't seen any boats come in other than the ferry all day. Her dad asked where we'd sailed from. I told him about our trip from Chicago.

The cute girl asked, "Where are you going?"

"We are sailing around the world," I replied.

"No way!" she said.

"Yes way."

I had to admit, I felt cool saying that. My dad came up from below and started talking to the other dad. They seemed to love talking about boats and my dad invited them onboard *Imagine* for a tour. After a while, we were invited to their cottage for dinner. The invitation was good news for mom, as I think she was ready to talk with other grown-ups. My mom likes to talk a lot. It was also good news for me, because the girl was a doll.

Their cottage was only about a half-mile away and an easy walk. We got there at about six that night. The cutie's name was Amanda. She was twelve. She asked me if I wanted to go down to the beach and I was all for that. One nice thing about Caroline was that she liked to hang with the old people, so it was just Amanda and I.

Down on the beach, we gathered several small rocks and built a fire pit for a little marshmallow roast later that night. I skipped some rocks in the lake and she collected wildflowers for her mom. We didn't talk much, but that was okay. She asked me how old I was and I exaggerated just a little and said, "Thirteen."

We stayed on the beach for almost an hour before heading back up to the house. The house sat on a bluff, so we had to walk up a long set of steps. Amanda was in front of me and about every third or fourth step, she would make little spins and then continue on like a ballet dancer. I asked her what was with all the little turns and she said she hadn't noticed and smiled. Man, she was cute.

By the time we got back to the house, I was starving. I was also looking forward to eating in a real room after three days in a small tube. On the table was a plate with crackers and cheese, another with small pieces of bread with tomatoes and something else on them, and some peanuts in a fancy bowl. It all looked nice, but not exactly what I was hoping for as a dinner. My mom explained that after the appetizers, we were all going down to the Beaver Island Lodge for a drink and then out to a place called Stoney Acre Grill for dinner. Amanda's mom had told my mom that the place had a shrimp dish to die for.

After dinner, we went back to the cottage for what my parents called "a night cap" and a little bonfire on the beach. We roasted marshmallows and told stories until the grown-ups decided to head up to the house. We kids were told we could stay at the beach for about another half-hour. I had to ask myself if Amanda and I were destined to meet. Life was good. Well, I thought it was good because I assumed that Caroline would hang with the adults. This time, for some unknown reason, she stayed at the beach with Amanda and me.

"Caroline," I asked, "aren't you going with Mom and Dad?"

"No," she replied. "I'll just hang with you guys."

That was bad news for me. She always hung with the adults, so why did she have to hang around this time? Something deep down inside told me I had a good chance of kissing my first girl. Chances were not so great with my ten-year-old sister hanging around.

I tried again, "Caroline, you always go with the adults."

"No, I don't" was her quick reply.

I looked at Amanda and she looked back as if confirming, "It could have been." Now that hurt.

The three of us sat there, roasting a few more marshmallows but not talking much. A ten-year-old pest had closed my window of opportunity. We covered the fire with sand and marched up the forty-two steps back to the house. At around midnight, Mom, Dad, Caroline and I were walking back to the boat. Our parents were holding hands as we walked. Caroline was holding my mom's other hand and asking her some dumb question about gravity and light. I was seemingly alone, wondering only about what could have been on the beach that night.

The next morning at five-thirty sharp, my dad started the engine. I knew what that meant for me—no more sleep and no more Amanda. That part of sailing was going to take me a while to get used to. Why we had to leave so early was beyond me.

As we pulled away from the dock, the sun was just coming up over the horizon. I looked back toward the island and could only imagine how sad Amanda must be. We had only the one night, and had my dad not been in his usual "keep moving" mode, our destiny of going together would have been a reality rather than a missing memory.

We were again under sail, racing along at a pitiful seven knots. Beaver Island stayed in view for about three hours until we made it to Mackinac Straights, heading for Lake Huron. Going through the straights, we passed under one of the largest suspension bridges in the world, the Mackinac Bridge. Also pretty cool was the fact we were being passed by an eight-hundred-foot freighter only thirty yards from the side of our boat at the same time.

As we went under, it looked as though our mast, which stuck up about sixty-five feet, would hit the bridge. Instead, we passed under, looking up through the open grates of the bridge at the cars above. The whole thing seemed almost make-believe, the four of us on this little boat heading toward the same ocean as the big freighter. Crazy.

Lake Huron was almost as long as Lake Michigan and it would take another three days and nights of nonstop sailing to reach St. Mary's River. Just after the bridge, however, we got a little surprise.

The channel was clearly marked showing a path about ten degrees to starboard. Rather than make that slight course adjustment, my dad turned the boat to port and headed toward an island. Even from a few miles away, we could see a huge hotel that I later learned was the Grand Hotel, which supposedly held claim to the longest porch in the world. After sailing past and continuing for another half-mile, we turned into the Mackinac Island Marina. Normally, my dad keeps to his "keep moving" schedule, so we were shocked by the unannounced stop. Shocked but happy.

The island allows no cars other than an ambulance and fire truck, so transportation is all by horse and carriage. After taking care of marina details, we were off to explore. Our first stop was one of the island's famous fudge shops, after which we rented four bikes and rode around. Following an easy two-hour bike ride, my dad took us to a horse livery.

None of us had any idea what he was doing until he came out with a guy who, after looking us over, said, "Follow me. We'll pick out your ride."

Our "ride" turned out to be our own horses. My mom was pretty excited—she used to ride as a kid. A couple of years earlier, our parents had taken us to a dude ranch in Durango Colorado, so Caroline and I had had some training. It was all too cool.

My horse was what is called a "paint," Caroline got a smaller brown horse with a white diamond on his nose, and my parents were given almost identical black horses. After a short briefing from the guide, we were off. My dad had rented the horses for two hours, so he took off for the interior of the island. We had already seen the outer part on the bikes.

Once we were away from the town, we came into a large meadow. My mom and dad picked up the pace to a gallop with Caroline right behind. I nudged my horse with my heels but got nothing in response. I kicked him again—still no response. I shook the reins, whacked him on the butt, but ended up with just the same slow walk. It was embarrassing. My whole family was on the other side of the meadow waiting as my stupid horse sauntered across, with no intention of picking up the pace. That same pathetic, lazy attitude continued for the next hour. I wondered if I could get a refund for getting the laziest horse in North America.

Finally, on the way back to the barn, my beast showed a little enthusiasm. I hadn't even nudged him and he started to gallop for the heck of it. I quickly took the lead and before I knew it I was going a lot faster than planned. I got nervous and pulled back on the reins, yelling, "Whoa, boy."

When I turned around to look back, I could see that I had left the others in the dust. I could faintly hear my mom yelling, "Tommy, slow down!" I had every intention of slowing down, but clearly my horse hadn't been to horse school because he didn't understand anything I tried to tell him. I pulled a little harder on the reins, but rather than slow, he suddenly—for no apparent reason—exited stage right onto a trail I hadn't even seen. I thought that what happened next would be the last thing that ever happened to me.

Somehow, with the sharp right turn, I slid halfway off the saddle to the left. My feet ended up higher than my head and I was looking up at the underside of the horse, watching his legs move at full speed. If my right foot hadn't been caught in the stirrup, I would have been on the ground—a place I would have rather been at that point. Instead, all I could do was hang on. I had to keep my head close to his belly so it wouldn't be cracked open by the trees as we passed them at a hundred miles an hour. The ground rushed by and my horse's legs looked as though they were still picking up speed.

Finally, just when I was about to believe I had no chance of surviving, the ground below me started to slow and the horse stopped dead in his tracks. From my awkward position, I couldn't see much. Looking up I saw only horse, and looking down there was only ground. Then I heard a man's voice from about a foot or two away. "Son, it's best to ride the horse right side up."

The guy must have thought he was a comedian. He helped me out of the stirrup and lifted me to the ground. My first thought was to find a gun and shoot the horse. My second thought was to see if I still had all my parts. This cowboy-looking guy took the reins, spit out some chewing tobacco, and asked, "Have a good ride, boy?" Which prompted my third thought—to shoot him after the horse.

My dad arrived next, followed by Caroline and my mom. My mom jumped off her horse and ran over, asking if I was okay. It had taken them so long to catch up that I had been able to gather my wits and replied, "Sure, Mom, I was just foolin' around." I looked at my horse and he stared back with his huge black eyes. He was lucky I didn't have a baseball bat.

When we arrived back at *Imagine*, I realized it was the first time I'd been excited to start sailing again. Mackinac Island could keep its fudge and dim-witted horses; I had a globe to explore.

We were off early the next morning and with good winds, it only took two-and-a-half days to get to Port Huron, Michigan, at the south end of Lake Huron. The lake ends at St. Clair River.

As we passed under the Blue Water Bridge, the current was running at about six knots, so our boat was moving at about twelve knots with the combined boat speed and current. Seeing the shore pass by so quickly made me feel as though I was on a real boat. Our original plan had been to stop and spend a night, but because it was early in the morning when we arrived, my dad, "Captain No Fun," decided to keep going all the way to Detroit.

The only good news was that the current was in our favor, making the trip to Detroit faster. Even a few miles downriver from the bridge, the current was still pushing us an extra two knots. It doesn't sound like much, but we went from motoring at six knots to actually making eight knots.

After exiting the St. Clair River, we sailed across the much smaller St. Clair Lake and into the Detroit River. My dad called ahead on the radio and got us a slip at the Detroit Yacht Club.

The club, located on Belle Isle, was great. The whole island is essentially a park with a lot to do. The yacht club had a large swimming pool and the added bonus of a lot of other kids.

Right away, I met a super-cool kid named Brian. He knew everyone at the club—or perhaps I should say that everyone at the club knew him. He also knew a lot about sailing. His dad raced their sailboat all the time and sometimes Brian raced with him. He introduced his parents to mine and they hit it off right away. His mom was a lot of fun and acted as if she'd known us her whole life. She invited us onto their boat and treated us like long-lost friends.

Caroline sat next to my mom in their cockpit and I stayed on the dock with Brian. Out of the blue, a bird landed on Brian's bare foot. He looked at it for a few seconds and then simply reached down and picked it up in his hand. I was amazed. The bird didn't look hurt or anything. It just sat in his hand for a minute or two and then flew away. Caroline was more than amazed. I was pretty sure I heard her tell my mom she was going to marry Brian someday. I think she saw him as some kind of "bird whisperer" or something. Anyway, from that moment on, she followed Brian around like a puppy.

It didn't take long for the four adults to make dinner plans together. Brian told his mom that he and I would take care of ourselves for dinner. His mom replied, "No, Brian, you're going to eat with us."

Brian looked at me and said, "Don't worry, Tommy. I can handle this."

He was right. Once the parents got talking at the club bar, they pretty much forgot about us.

"Come on, Tommy," Brian said. "Let's go get dinner."

"Can I come with you guys?" Caroline asked. (What she meant was, "Can I come with *you*, Brian?")

I said no and Brian said sure, so Caroline came with us.

I wasn't sure how we were going to get dinner given I had no money, and I was pretty sure Brian didn't, either. We went to an outside grill and were seated by a hostess as if we were adults. The waiter came over and Brian started to order. I asked him how we would pay for it and he told me to relax. He knew his parents' club membership number and with that bit of information it seemed we could order whatever we wanted, which we did. I had the best cheeseburger ever.

We drank virgin strawberry daiquiris and talked football. Brian knew everything there was to know about the NFL. Caroline didn't say much. She looked as if she were just waiting for another bird to land on Brian. We had a great time and, as it turned out, I really didn't mind Caroline being there. Besides, when the bill came, she quickly calculated the tip for us. Brian filled in the amount, filled his parents' account number in, signed his name, and we were set to go.

Unfortunately, we were only staying one night on Belle Isle. My dad had been clear that we would be off early in the morning, as usual. Brian and I exchanged e-mails and agreed to try to get together again someday. There had already been talk of his parents coming to see us in the Caribbean when we got there.

As we walked down the dock to our boat, Caroline turned back and said, "'Bye, Brian. Thank you for dinner."

She was only ten, but it seemed she had her first crush.

The next morning, as predicted, the motor started up at five-thirty sharp. This time we were heading to Lake Erie. The plan was to not make anymore stops until Lake Ontario. Getting from Lake Erie to Lake Ontario requires going through the Welland Canal, which has a system that lowers boats from the higher Lake Erie to the lower Lake Ontario. Our boat had to move through a series of chambers called locks, which took most of the day. The process was simple. You drive the boat into a lock and loosely tie up to the side. Then a big gate closes behind you and water is let out to lower the boat. Once lowered, a gate in front opens and you motor through into the next one. We did this several times and dropped over two hundred feet in all. The only other option would be to go over Niagara Falls!

In the first lock, it seemed like no big deal. In fact, it seemed as if nothing happened. I learned how things really worked in lock two. We pulled in, loosely tied to the side, and waited. I figured we had time, given that we had been in the previous lock for about fifteen minutes, so I decided to take a little stroll. Turned out this is a no-no.

As I walked around in search of a vending machine, I noticed that only the top of our mast was still visible in the lock. I ran over to see our boat over forty feet below me! My dad yelled, "Tommy, what are you doing up there?"

I really had no answer. I stood and watched as the gate in front of the boat opened and *Imagine* moved into the next chamber, beyond the point where I could get on board. After a little time on the radio, my dad arranged for the lock control people to find another boat coming through behind us and talk someone into letting me ride with them.

I ended up on a cool boat. It was a sailboat like ours, but it had two masts and was about twice as long. The best thing about it was a big flat-screen TV in the cabin. Now this was a sailboat! Because I had departed *Imagine* in only the second lock, I spent most the day with the Wheelers. At first, I had assumed I would re-join our boat in the next lock, but it soon became clear that *Imagine* would remain one lock ahead for the entire trip through the canal.

Mr. Wheeler was a funny guy. He asked me for fifty dollars and said it was the standard fee for transporting stray boys. Since I had only a couple of dollars, he said, "Well, boy, then I guess you have work to do."

He put me in charge of handling one of the lines that got passed down from the lock people. I had to keep tension on the line as the boat was lowered in the lock to keep it close to the wall. As we made our way through each chamber, Mr. Wheeler would call off how much debt had been reduced. Mrs. Wheeler was tending to the line on the bow and I stood at the middle of the boat—amidships.

She winked at me and said, "He's cruel but fair."

I looked back at the boss man and he pointed to the rope to let me know I had a job to do. It was actually fun spending the day with them. I would have liked to stay on their boat longer, given the flat-screen TV and all, but unfortunately I had to return to *Imagine*.

The two boats finally tied up together at the end of the locks and the grown-ups introduced themselves. As I stepped off their boat, Mr. Wheeler said, "Hey, Tommy, you forgot your pay."

"My pay?"

"Yes. You not only paid off your debt, but you made six dollars."

Overall, it turned out to be a pretty good day. My dad didn't even yell at me, but my mom gave me "that look."

I climbed aboard *Imagine*, my dad gave thanks to the Wheelers, and we carried on into Lake Ontario. It would take us a couple of days, but the next stop would be the great St. Lawrence Seaway.

FIVE

We entered the St. Lawrence Seaway exactly four weeks after we left Chicago. This was the large river that would deliver us to the Atlantic Ocean in about another five hundred miles.

Canada is on the north side of the river, and on the south is the United States. Once in the seaway, our first stop was a small yacht club in Clayton, New York. I was off the boat in a flash, ready for some real people and to walk more than forty-six feet in one direction.

I made my way to a small outdoor hamburger place for my first off-the-boat meal in three days. Just as I arrived, a mean-looking, six-foot-tall guy came out and kicked a big black dog right in the ribs. The dog yelped and took off along the river. I gave the guy a shocked look and he said, "That mutt's always hanging around begging. He's a pest."

He was such a jerk and I really felt bad for the dog. I ordered a double hamburger with no bun, a second regular cheeseburger, and some fries. The guy looked at me a bit strange given the odd order, but not as strangely as when he watched me take my two beef patties to the dog. He eyed me in obvious anger as the dog ate the burgers while I sat next to the pooch eating my cheeseburger. Perhaps when he saw me sharing my fries, it became too much to bear. He came out the front door and marched right over to me, looking pretty ticked off. I was sure my ribs were next.

"Get out of here, you little rat. You're just making that mutt worse!"

He stepped a bit closer and raised his hand in a threatening way. When he was just a couple of feet away, I started to close my eyes in anticipation of the pain about to come my way when the big black dog rose up and stood between me and the human beast.

The dog stood right in front of me, growling, almost daring the guy to take a shot. The loser got quiet and started backing away, the dog's eyes fixed on him the whole time. Once he figured he was a safe distance away, he ran back into the store. I was stunned. The dog sat next to me again and gave me a little lick on the cheek.

I hadn't even finished my burger but thought it best to move on. Who knew what the psycho in the burger place might do next? I jogged back to the boat and the dog followed.

"Whose dog?" my mom asked.

"I don't know, but I'm pretty sure he doesn't belong to the guy from the hamburger joint."

The next morning as we were getting ready to shove off, to my surprise the dog was still on the dock, so before taking off I gave him a bowl of warm oatmeal and a slice of toast with peanut butter. He seemed to love it. I gave him a pat on the head and a little hug around the neck, which prompted a sloppy kiss on the face in return.

Back on the boat, after the usual routine of casting off lines, we pulled out of the dock and headed back out into the St. Lawrence River. The dog ran along the dock as if to say, "Hey, take me with you." My guess is that if he knew the whole story regarding our little family adventure, he would have just waved and said, "Good luck. See ya."

I was ready to take a little nap after about four hours of sailing downstream. As I headed down the companionway, something caught my eye on shore. A big black dog was running with his tongue hanging out, moving in the same direction and at the same speed as the boat.

"Strange," I thought, "another big black dog. They must grow here."

That night, we stayed on the Canadian side of the river. My dad preferred not to sail at night in the river because of all the ships passing through. We stood the night at anchor, so we were not able to get to shore. We were back on the U.S. side the next night.

If I hadn't been there myself, I would have never believed it. The dog—the big black dog from Clayton—walked up to the boat, looking exhausted. He sat down and looked up at me.

My mom said, "Tommy, that looks a lot like the dog from Clayton."

"It is the dog from Clayton, Mom."

I got the dog some water and made him a peanut-butter-and-jelly sandwich. I told my parents what had happened back at the burger stand.

My dad's first thought was to go back to have a talk with the fellow making the burgers, but then he questioned how the dog could have come so far.

The dog looked tired and weak. I asked my dad if we could bring him onboard for the night, but the answer was a firm no.

At least I could be sure he would have some food in the morning if he hung out again overnight.

Sure enough, that was the case. The next morning, he was sitting right next to *Imagine*. I made him another big bowl of oatmeal and a peanut-butter–and-jelly sandwich. I also threw in a peanut butter cookie, which he devoured in about two seconds. He seemed to like peanut butter. I gave the dog one last hug before leaving him a second time.

Imagine and her crew were off once again to the great St. Lawrence. Our next stop was Montreal. We spent two nights there, tied up in the city basin. People would come down to the shops along the harbor and look at the boats. I would wave, most would wave back, and some would even come by and talk. Most didn't believe that we were sailing around the world. Why would they? I didn't, either.

We then headed to Quebec City. It was on this section of river, between Montreal and Quebec City, that my life changed forever. Approaching Quebec we crossed the Rideau Rapids, a narrow area of river with a six-knot current. Two boats could barely go through at the same time. As we started into the rapids, a large freighter was coming in the opposite direction. The combined speed of our boat with the current had us moving at thirteen knots.

I made a big mistake. When we were in water conditions like this, my dad insisted that we wear life jackets. I had left mine drying on the rail on the back of the boat. I stepped out of the cockpit, moved ten feet to the back of the boat to fetch my jacket, and *splash.* I tripped on a line and went right over the stern rail into the St. Lawrence River. No life jacket, and—worse—me streaming out of control toward the approaching freighter!

The whole thing felt like it happened in slow motion. *Imagine* was moving quickly away and I could see the frantic look on my dad's face. True fear. My mom was screaming. There they were, with no way to turn the boat around. The ship coming up the other way was one issue, and the other was that the channel was far too narrow for my dad to make a turn. With the current, *Imagine* was on a one-way trip. My mom was trying to signal the freighter as if there was something they could do. They certainly couldn't turn, either.

I started swimming as hard as I could toward the shore. After several strokes, I was pretty sure I wouldn't make it. The freighter would run me over and spit me back out in a hundred pieces. The odd thing was, I remember thinking how hard it was going to be for my mom. Odd because it seemed as though I should have been more concerned about how *I* would feel about being dead!

I put my head down kicked and pulled with all I had. I turned my head for a breath and saw something black running along the shore out of the corner of my eye. As I stroked with all my worth, the big black dog leapt off a ledge about fifteen feet above the water. I couldn't think about anything other than what it was going to feel like when the freighter hit me until I felt the dog next to me. He grabbed the side of my shorts with his teeth and swam with power you couldn't imagine. I stroked and kicked, and with the dog's help, my speed was amazing. I felt as though he was steering me toward the shore and away from the ship.

As the freighter approached, I could feel the water pulling me into the ship's hull only a few feet away. I thought I was about to get sucked in when I felt a surge from the dog, and then suddenly I was free from the pull of the ship. However, I was also now free of the dog and saw him disappear under the stern of the massive ship.

As I got closer to shore, the current got surprisingly less strong. I could see rocks in the shallower water and managed to climb onto one. I sat down for a moment, more exhausted than I thought humanly possible. I looked and looked for the dog, but he was nowhere to be seen. I had watched him disappear under the ship, so I guess I knew he was dead.

I didn't want to know this. I had never felt that kind of sadness—I didn't even know anything could be that sad. I couldn't even cry. It seemed there was nothing left in me.

But I was alive.

Our boat came into view about a mile down the river. My dad had pulled over to the right of the channel. He was circling, trying to hold the boat's position in the river. There was no way to communicate with my parents. I wasn't even sure they knew where I was. Most likely, they would be looking farther down the river. I tried to stand and signal, but my legs just wouldn't cooperate. If I tried to stand, my legs would just give out. So I just sat there, hoping to be noticed. It was a bit of a change for me, as usually I hoped for the opposite—if my parents were looking for me, I was usually in trouble.

A red flare shot off the stern of *Imagine*. About two minutes later, there was another. The red streaks went up about two hundred feet. I had never seen an emergency flare launched before. It felt a little strange knowing I was the reason for the display.

It didn't take long before a lot of activity was going on around our boat. In the distance, I could see three small boats going back and forth across the river, clearly looking for me. They got farther away as they searched farther down the river.

After about a half hour, I thought my best bet was to jump back into the river and try to swim for the boat. The only problem was that if my legs couldn't even hold me up, the swim might not go all that well.

Another freighter passed by, this time going downriver. I waved with both arms but could not tell if anyone could see me. I never actually saw anyone, but the ship was only about one hundred yards away. It continued on its way and was gone in no time.

It was strange having the feeling of being saved when I climbed up on the rock, but then wondering if it were actually true. No one knew where I was. I believed that when my strength came back, I could make it to shore. The only problem was I didn't know how far down the river I would have to swim before I would find a place that wasn't too high to climb. The dog had jumped from a long way up.

This kind of decision making was a lot more difficult than my normal "Do I bunt or go for the homer?" I remembered my father once saying, "If you're safe out of the water, don't go back in." I figured it was time to listen for a change, so the rock was my new home for the time being.

After about another fifteen minutes, just when I thought things were hopeless, I saw a small boat with an outboard motor coming upriver right toward me. As it got closer, I could see my dad standing in the front with binoculars, looking right at me.

I hate to admit it, but I started to cry. I focused on pulling it together because I sure didn't want to be crying when my dad got there. I also started thinking about the dog—the great, amazing, lifesaving dog—that I would never see again. My brain had never been pushed around like that. I just wanted to get back into my port-side sea birth and never leave it again.

The small boat pulled alongside the rock. My dad jumped into the water, climbed up, and held me like never before. "Are you okay?" he asked.

I said, "Yes, Dad, I'm fine."

We got in the boat and sped back downstream to *Imagine.* My mom was crying; so was Caroline. At least for now, I wasn't. We climbed up the swim ladder and I was safe back on our boat—my home.

My mom hugged me to a point that I couldn't breathe. We all stood there for a while until Caroline took my hand and said, "Come with me." She led me down the companionway to her cabin.

As soon as she opened the door, it was all over for me. The tears just poured out. I cried like a baby. There was the dog, lying on Caroline's bed. He lifted his head and looked at me, but was unable to get up. I stood there for a moment in disbelief, but then jumped on him. Never had I been so happy.

Caroline explained, "We saw the dog jump into the river and go to you. None of us could believe what we saw. Then when Dad was searching the river, he found the dog along the shore. He pulled him into the fishing boat and actually gave him CPR."

"How do you give a dog CPR?" I asked.

"He pumped the dog's chest, then held the dog's mouth closed and put his own mouth around the dog's nose. He blew air into the dog. He did it about five times. Then the dog just coughed up water and started breathing. He dropped the dog on our boat and kept searching for you."

I could hardly believe what I was hearing.

She continued, "Mom and I brought him into my cabin. I have been taking care of him since."

"How did Dad know where I was?"

"I could hear him on the radio after he brought the dog onboard. A freighter passing by told him they saw a boy on a rock upriver waving his arms."

"Wow," I thought, "they *had* seen me signal."

My parents came into the room. We all just looked at each other. No words, just silence. I wasn't even in trouble.

"Can we keep him?" I asked.

I was shocked when my dad replied, "We need to sort some things out first. For starters, we need to contact folks in Clayton to see if anyone is missing their dog."

"So if there is no one, he can stay?"

"Well, we really have no choice since we can't seem to shake him. Besides, I've already named him."

"What?" I asked.

"After watching how he changed your direction in the water to keep you clear of the ship, I decided to call him 'Rudder.'"

Six

Because it was late, we couldn't make it to Quebec City before night, so my dad picked a new place outside the channel to anchor. Rudder was looking better. His tail started to move and he got up from lying on his side to a more upright position. I knew just what he needed. I made him some oatmeal and mixed in some peanut butter. He didn't seem too interested in any water…can't say I blamed him.

Caroline let me sleep in her cabin that night. We slept with Rudder between us. In the morning, my dad woke me in the usual way as if nothing had happened the day before. Rudder wasn't in the bed.

"Dad, where is Rudder?"

"On deck, doing your job."

I put on some fresh clothes and headed up to the cockpit. Rudder was up on the bow. It seemed he knew what had to be done and was waiting for me. My first job was to man the anchor chain. There were two buttons on the bow that operated the chain—one for up, one for down. On my dad's order, I stepped on the Up button and watched the chain come up. I gave my dad hand signals so he would know which way to steer the boat so the anchor would come up clean.

Approaching Quebec City from the river was cool. The tides there were over eighteen feet, so the marina was located in a harbor behind a lock. If you arrived at high tide, you had to go into the lock and be lowered about nine feet before entering the marina harbor, and vice versa at low tide. People stood on both sides of the lock gates and watched the boats come through. I could tell Rudder enjoyed having his picture taken by the tourists.

After securing a place on the dock, my dad had to go into the Canadian Customs office. He took all our passports and the boat papers. When he returned, there was a Customs officer with him. It was about Rudder. We had no papers for the dog. Who would guess a dog needed papers?

My dad explained that we had picked up the dog as a stray in the United States. He also explained that we had already called the yacht club in Clayton where we'd found the dog, and that we had taken out an ad in the local paper looking for the owner. The agent wasn't mean or anything, he just had his job to do.

There was no fighting City Hall. The officer was clear that the dog would have to be in quarantine for two weeks. Not only did he have to be quarantined, he had to be at the Customs facility in a cage.

Dog jail, in other words. This was bad news. First, Rudder would hate it; second, my dad planned to be in Nova Scotia within the next two weeks. Nova Scotia was another eight hundred miles away, and with a couple of planned stops, it would take about two weeks to get there. My dad was not too keen on changing plans and hanging around in Quebec. It seemed unlikely that I would get to keep Rudder after all.

None of us knew for sure what my dad would do. We waited to see how he would respond to the Customs agent's demand or the idea of a big delay. We were amazed. He calmly looked at Rudder and said, "You're not going to like this, boy." He kneeled down next to him and added, "But we will all be here with you."

He tied a short rope around Rudder's neck and walked him up the dock to his new home for the next two weeks.

Each day, Caroline and I would be at the dog jail first thing in the morning. They fed him well, but I would still take him his favorite: a peanut-butter–and-jelly sandwich on wheat bread. I thought it helped take the edge off prison life.

During those two weeks, my dad stayed busy during the day doing boat stuff. He was always fixing something. My mom was always walking around Old Town. She really liked Quebec and Old Town. There were art galleries and nice restaurants all over the place.

She loved two things: fine art and eating in fancy restaurants. We had been moving so much that she rarely had the opportunity since we left Chicago. Now that we were staying put for a couple of weeks, she made it clear that there was time.

For the first time ever, my parents left my sister and me alone while they went to dinner. Not even at home in the real world did we ever stay alone. We always had a sitter. This time, the rules were simple: life jackets when out of the cabin, no other people on the boat, and no killing each other!

Our parents stayed out until sometime after midnight. It was strange, us kids waiting up for the parents. We spotted them coming up the walking trail alongside the marina. They were walking slow and holding hands. The lights along the path were just bright enough that we could see it was actually them. It was clear that they were in no hurry to see if their children were still alive. To my shock, only about a hundred feet from the entrance to our dock, they sat on a bench. What happened next almost caused me to go blind. They started making out! Yes, our two insane parents were making out in public on a park bench!

Caroline said, "Isn't that romantic?"

"Romantic my butt," I replied. "That's just gross. Parents aren't supposed to make out, they're supposed to... Well, I don't know. But they're not supposed to make out!"

Obviously, it was time for me to head to my space, and that's just what I did.

The next morning, I was very excited. Finally, the time had come to get Rudder. There had been no word from anyone in Clayton, so Rudder would be a permanent member of the Tiller family.

Dad had to pay some fees for vaccinations and stuff, but we ended up with a full set of papers for Rudder. He was now legal and had a last name: Tiller.

As we walked back to the dock, he wagged his tail and smiled all the way to *Imagine*. When we arrived, he jumped from the dock to the bow and stood there as if to tell anyone and everyone that this was his boat and he was home.

My dad had to time our departure with the currents created by the tide coming in and going out. This meant leaving Quebec later in the day sailing overnight. Our next stop was clean out of the St. Lawrence River in the Gulf of St. Lawrence. My dad said this was part of the Atlantic Ocean. I couldn't believe it. It didn't seem very long ago that we were in Chicago. Now, come morning, we would be in the Atlantic Ocean.

The ship traffic was busy as we sailed down the last leg of the river. It was fun seeing all the different flags from various countries on the ships. My mom had an application on her computer that showed all the flags, so it was fun to identify them.

Caroline and I played a game of country identification by flag and used the computer for confirmation. It was fun at first, but when the score reached Caroline eight, Tommy three, I decided the game was dumb. Besides, the girl was a freak. She even knew the flag for Tunisia. I didn't even know there was a Tunisia.

After a nice lunch, I looked toward the stern and noticed Rudder making circles on the deck. "Uh-oh," I thought, "I know what's going to happen."

"Ah, Mom, I think Rudder is going to have an accident on the stern," I said.

"No problem," my mom replied. "He knows just what he's doing."

She gave him a couple minutes and then patted him on the head and said, "Good boy, Rudder."

The day before we left Quebec, my mom had gone to a sporting goods store and bought some Astroturf. It looks just like grass. It was an area about two by four feet with a small rope tied to one end. After Rudder did his business, my mom just tossed the turf overboard for a rinse and pulled it back onboard, ready for the next time. Pretty cool.

My dad called me over to the helm. He wanted to show me his plan for the night. We would sail about eight hours and then find a place to anchor for four hours or so. This was all because of the strong currents caused by the tide coming in and out called the flood and ebb.

He was explaining that if we tried to sail against the flood when the tide was coming in, our boat speed would only be about two knots—not really worth the effort. If we waited until the flood slowed and then used the ebb, we could sail around ten knots. Sounded good to me.

Around two a.m., we pulled out of the channel into a cove off a small island. Rudder and I took our positions on the bow and readied the anchor. On my dad's command, we sent it to the bottom. We let out about one hundred and fifty feet of chain, felt the anchor grab the bottom, and returned to the cockpit, like the anchor pros we were. Once my dad was confident that the anchor had a good hold, we went below for a nap.

As tired as I was, I couldn't sleep. I could hear the water moving quickly under the boat and knew something was wrong. We had to be moving. I went up to the cockpit. It was so dark that I couldn't see a thing. The boat speed indicator read six knots! Holy smokes! Not only were we moving, we were moving at six knots!

I raced down the companionway into my parents' room. "Dad, the boat's moving!" I screamed.

My dad popped up like a jack-in-the-box. "Are you sure?" he said.

"Yes," I replied anxiously. "We're moving at six knots."

My dad shot up to the helm and yelled, "Tommy, man the anchor."

I headed forward, but my dad changed orders. "Never mind, Tommy. You can go back to bed."

I looked at him in disbelief. "What do you mean, go back to bed? What about the anchor?"

"Don't worry, it has a good set," he said.

"But—"

"The six knots you see on the knot meter is just the current moving under the boat. We aren't actually moving."

Boy, did I feel dumb. In my embarrassment, I asked, "Do you think we can keep this between the two of us?"

He smiled. "Tommy, you did everything right."

"Right?" I asked.

"Yes. First, you were alert to the sound change. Second, you went up to the cockpit for a look. In the darkness, you couldn't see land for reference. You thought the boat was moving, so the only thing you could have done wrong would have been not to get me. I'm proud of you."

At that point I was thinking, "Forget about keeping it between us, tell Mom and Caroline!"

I got excited as the sun came up. This was the day we would exit the St. Lawrence for the great Atlantic Ocean. I wasn't sure I believed we would actually make it to an ocean, but here we were with just twenty miles to go. Our first port of call would be the Canadian town of Tadoussac on the banks of the Saguenay River. According to my mom, this is the only natural fjord on the North American mainland.

I guess what makes it a fjord is that, unlike a river that flows out to the sea, in this case the sea is flowing into the land. In other words, it's like a river going backward. I'm not sure why it matters. To me, it just looked like a regular river.

One cool thing about this area was that there were whales all over the place. By seven in the morning, we were all on deck. My mom was so excited. She was taking pictures like crazy as whale after whale surfaced by our boat. For the first time, I felt like part of something big. Two huge creatures swam side by side next to us. It was easy to tell they were a couple. I could also tell they were aware of us and were fine with sharing their waters. It was then when I first realized I no longer missed not having a TV.

Caroline screamed, "Mom, look! Belugas over there, four of them."

My mom was shooting pictures as fast as she could aim. I had no idea what Caroline was talking about at the time. Later, I found out that belugas are rare white whales.

We must have seen thirty whales that morning. One humpback whale was only about ten feet from the side of our boat and was at least ten feet longer than *Imagine*. It was cool, but I think the whales made my dad a little nervous. He had told me before that whales can damage a boat, sometimes by accident and sometimes not. They have been known to attack boats, but only when they feel threatened. I kept this in mind the whole time and hoped they never felt threatened.

Once we were comfortably anchored in the bay, Rudder climbed in the dinghy and we headed for shore. I tried to talk to a guy at the dock to make sure it was okay to tie off there, but he only spoke French. I tried another guy—again, only French. Eventually I just pointed to our dinghy and put my hand up with the okay sign, and he nodded his head in approval. "Come on, boy, we're good to go," I said to Rudder.

In each new place we visited, I had a mission. My mom would send me as a scout to find out if there was any free Wi-Fi so we could get e-mails and weather information, and to search for a place to do laundry. It was more fun now having Rudder to help me. We lucked out and located both. Rudder enjoyed using some real grass for his business, and then we were back off to the mother ship to report our findings.

SEVEN

The next morning, we pulled anchor and started up the Saquenay. My parents had decided to take a detour to a place called The Bay of Eternity, about twenty miles up the river.

The trip was amazing. There were mountains on both sides going straight up and waterfalls coming from so high that you couldn't tell where they started. Dolphins and seals swam around the boat. It was like another planet. My parents would just look at each other and smile. I was hoping they wouldn't start making out again.

When we reached our destination, the water was too deep to anchor. In fact, with the boat just twenty feet from shore, the water was over two hundred feet deep. Luckily, the Bay of Eternity was a Canadian National Park, so it had mooring balls set that we could tie to.

The mooring balls were nice. There were big concrete blocks on the bottom and then thick rope hooked to the block. The rope was held on the surface by large floating balls. We picked up a ball, grabbed the rope, and tied it to our boat. Presto—anchored with no anchor.

We settled in and dad made a great lunch. He even made an extra serving for Rudder.

My dad, Mom, Caroline, Rudder, and I sat in the cockpit looking up at the mountains and waterfalls. You didn't see this in Chicago.

There were few people in the bay and only two other boats. My dad wanted us to go for a hike and we were all up for that. We put on our hiking shoes, packed a few essentials in a backpack, and loaded into the dinghy.

When we got to shore, we hiked about a half-mile to a little information building. It had a small restaurant and gift shop. Outside, about ten people were gathered around looking frantic and shouting to each other. Something was clearly wrong. My dad asked what all the commotion was about, and the lady at the counter explained a four-year-old girl had gone missing.

It was clear who the mom was. She was about twenty feet away and crying like no tomorrow. A guy who looked to be only about sixteen was directing people for the search. They all seemed young. I couldn't help but wonder where all the grown-ups were.

Apparently, the mom had come up for the day by car with her four-year-old and two other kids who were about seven and nine. The other teenagers milling around were an unrelated group of campers. They had called for park rangers, but no one knew how long it would take for help to come.

My dad went straight over to the crying woman to get more information. She pointed to a path where her daughter was last seen walking. The teenagers were already running down the path in search of her.

"Miss, are you sure she went down that path?" my dad asked.

She answered, "Yes, I'm sure, but I have looked up and down it and can't find her." She was crying so much it was hard to understand her.

"Do you have any clothes of hers, something that she has recently worn?"

The lady looked at him. "Why?"

"Look, it's important. Just tell me, do you?"

"Yes," she said, her lips quivering. "I have a shirt she wore yesterday."

This made her cry even harder. She reached into a shoulder bag, pulled out a small undershirt, and passed it to my dad. He turned to Rudder and held it in front of his nose

After about a five-second sniff, my dad looked Rudder in the eyes and said, "Find her, boy."

Rudder immediately had his nose glued to the ground. At first, it looked as though he was just going to go in circles but after a couple of circles he took off down the same path as all the teenagers in the search party. I started to follow, but then Rudder came right back to where we all stood.

It was something to see. Rudder stopped for a couple of seconds and put his nose up in the air and then back in the dirt. A few seconds later, he took off in the wrong direction! He wasn't going any- where near the path where the girl had last been seen.

He started into the woods—no path, just trees and brush. We couldn't see any footprints, so we didn't know what was going on with Rudder. When he would get too far ahead of us, he would turn around and rejoin but with a look of "Hurry up, you guys." Although he was clearly going in the wrong direction, my dad and I decided to follow.

After about ten minutes of going the wrong way, we came to an end. We were all standing at the edge of a cliff with nothing but a huge drop-off. We approached the edge and looked down. There was nothing but rocks and a small stream about thirty feet below. No girl, just a dead end.

My dad, anxious to get back to the real search, turned and began to head back the way we came. I followed close behind, but Rudder didn't move. He stayed on the cliff edge and barked.

My dad stopped, looked back at Rudder, and said, "Come on, boy."

Rudder didn't move. Instead, he turned the other way and looked down from the cliff.

My dad looked confused, but he slowly walked back to Rudder. "What is it, boy?" he said.

Rudder was down on all fours, looking over the cliff edge. My dad got on his belly and crawled up to the edge of the cliff next to Rudder. As he looked over, I was afraid he was going to fall off. He crawled back a couple of feet and said, "Tommy, get back to the dinghy as fast as you can. Get Caroline's life jacket out of the front compartment. Untie the rope from the dinghy anchor and bring the rope and life jacket back here. If you see any teenagers or adults, bring them. And Tommy, hurry."

I was off like no tomorrow. I got to the dinghy, got the gear, and was back up to the information center in no time, but there was no one around.

I knew I didn't have time to keep looking, so I bolted back through the woods to my dad. As soon as I got there, he said, "Tommy, is anyone else coming?"

"No, Dad, there wasn't anyone else."

My dad looked worried. "Okay," he said. "Here's what we're going to do." He unwrapped the rope. "Tommy, I don't think I can lower myself down there and then get back up with her, so I'm going to have to send you. Can you do it?"

"Sure I can," I replied.

My dad tied one end of the rope around a tree and tossed the other end over the ledge with Caroline's life jacket attached. "Tommy, are you sure?" he asked.

"Ya, I've got it. No problem, Dad."

"Now, once you get down there, put the life jacket on the girl and then tie the rope with several knots to the lanyard ring. Once you have her secure, I will pull her up and then send the rope back down to you. Got it?"

"Yep, I got it," I replied.

I got on my belly and crawled backward toward the ledge. When I got closer, my dad said, "Now listen, when you get to the bottom, you're going to be in water about ankle deep. Don't worry."

"Dad, there is only a little stream and no water where I will land."

"The tide is coming in, so the whole valley down there is flooding. In another hour, it will be six feet deep." he replied.

"Wow," I thought to myself. "*This* I didn't know."

As my feet and legs passed over the edge, my dad looked me right in the eye. "Son, are you sure?"

"Of course. I'll be down and back in a jiffy."

My dad watched as I disappeared over the ledge. I think he was nervous. It seemed like a long way down. After what felt like forever, my feet met ground, and, just as my dad had said, I was ankle deep in water.

I was right next to the little girl. My dad yelled down, "Is she breathing?"

I yelled back, "She's crying. She wants her mommy."

"Is she hurt?"

"Afraid so," I said. "She has a broken leg."

It didn't take a rocket scientist to figure that out. The end of the bone was sticking right out of her skin. I knelt down by her and said, "Don't worry, my dad's a doctor and he will fix you up."

Even as I said those words, I was actually pretty freaked out. I started sweating a lot and felt a little light-headed.

My dad shouted down, "Tommy, are you good?"

It took me a moment, but I yelled back, "Yep, I'm good."

"Put the life jacket on her and get her hooked up."

I remembered the ring on my jacket that had kept me from being washed overboard in the storm in Lake Michigan. Once I had the rope tied and double-tied, my dad said, "Okay, now help her up as I start lifting."

As I did, she really started to cry. "Dad, what about her leg?"

"Ignore it. Just get her up. We don't have much time."

The water was now almost up to my knees. I got her up and my dad started lifting.

I stood at the bottom and watched this little doll-looking thing get lifted to safety. It all looked good until she got to the top. My dad had to sit about three feet from the ledge to dig in his heels to lift her. When she got to the top, the life jacket caught on the ledge and kept her from getting over it.

I could hear my dad grunting, pulling with all his might, but she was stuck. Then I saw two black paws and a black head as Rudder leaned over and grabbed the jacket with his teeth, pulling her up and over.

The water was now well over my knees and my dad sent the line right back down. "Tommy, it's a long way up. Do you need me to pull you up?"

I replied, "I don't need a lift."

I grabbed the rope like in gym class and started climbing. It was farther than I had ever climbed before, but with the floodwater now approaching my waist, I was motivated. When I reached the top, I could see that my dad's hands were bleeding a little.

"Listen carefully," he said. "Go to the boat and grab the first-aid kit and the large red bag next to it."

"No problem," I said. "I'm on it."

As I started to run, my dad yelled, "Take Rudder with you and send him for Mom."

Rudder and I were on task and flying. We got to the information center. Again, no one was around. "Go get Mom," I told Rudder.

He took off down the path as though he knew exactly where he was going. I went the other direction, heading for the boat.

My job at this point was easy. I ran about a half-mile down the path to the dock and jumped into the dinghy. When I got to the boat, I knew exactly where to find the first-aid kit and, just as my dad had said, there was a larger red bag next to it. I collected the stuff and jumped back into the dinghy.

When I arrived back at the information center, there was no sign of Rudder or my mom. I knew my dad needed the first-aid kit pronto, so I took off to meet back up with him. When I got there, my mom was on her knees holding the little girl's head in her lap. Caroline was holding her hand and Rudder was just standing there with a look of "What took you so long?"

What happened next really freaked me out. My dad pulled out a clear bag filled with liquid. The bag was labeled Lactated Ringers—whatever the heck that was. He connected the bag to a clear tube.

Then came the first gross part. He unwrapped a needle and stuck it right in the girl's arm. After that, he connected the clear tube to the end of the needle so the liquid from the bag was going into her arm. The strange thing was, the girl didn't even cry. In fact, she made no sound at all. She stared blankly into my mother's eyes.

I figured this had been the worst part. I was wrong. My dad pulled out another clear bag, this one labeled Normal Saline. He cut the bottom off and poured the whole bag onto her bone and into the wound.

"Dad, what are you doing?"

"Her ankle is dislocated. The bone you see is the end of her tibia."

"But why are you squirting it with all that water?"

"We have to wash off as much debris as possible because I have to put her ankle back in position and we don't want any dirt in the joint."

I wasn't sure what he meant, but it didn't take long to find out.

"Tommy, come up here and hold her leg."

"What do you mean, hold her leg?"

"You're going to hold the upper part and I'm going to pull on her foot to get the bone back where it belongs."

Before I could ask any more questions, my dad was getting a hold of her foot. As I held her leg, my dad pulled. There was a horrible sucking sound followed by a *pop* as the end of her bone went out of sight, back over her foot where it belonged.

I felt a little dizzy. The girl screamed for just a second while Caroline held her hand and talked to her.

My mom smiled at my dad. He was working faster than I had ever seen him work. He pulled bandages and wraps out of the first-aid kit and had her ankle and leg wrapped before I even realized I could let go of her leg. He picked her up in his arms and started moving back toward the information center. Fortunately, this time, there was a man there who had just arrived in a ranger's truck.

As my dad held the girl, the ranger said, "Give her to me. I will take her to the hospital."

"Call a helicopter, this girl needs IV antibiotics immediately and there may be other internal injuries," my dad responded.

The ranger started to tell my dad again that he would drive her, but my dad wasn't having it.

"Listen, it's going to take you two to three hours by truck. That's too long. Call for a medevac chopper. They can start the antibiotics immediately when they get here and have her to the hospital in half the time."

The ranger could tell there was no arguing with my dad. He got on his radio and started the process of getting a chopper to take the little girl to a hospital.

Soon the girl's mom came running up. She was crying. I mean *really* crying. I thought she should be smiling, but she could hardly speak she was crying so hard. My dad carefully put the girl in her mom's arms. At first, I don't think she even realized the girl was hurt badly. My dad explained the situation and sure enough she cried even more. One odd thing was that even with her mom holding her, the little girl wouldn't let go of Caroline's hand.

About forty-five minutes later, we heard the helicopter coming our way. The ranger directed the pilot to a field close to the information center. We all walked toward the landed chopper and the medics ran out.

My dad explained the injury and gave some instructions. The medics plugged a bottle of antibiotics into the tube my dad had put in her arm. She was then placed on a stretcher, and she and her mom were loaded onto the helicopter while the big blade was still rotating.

The ranger told the mom he would bring her other two children to meet her at the hospital, and a couple of other people told her they would bring her car.

Just before the helicopter lifted off, I saw Caroline lean over to the little girl. It looked as though she was trying to tell Caroline something. Their hands finally separated and my sister walked back to the rest of us.

"What did she say to you?" I asked.

Caroline replied, "She asked me what your name was."

I replied, "Ya, and...?"

Caroline said, "I told her your name is Tommy Tiller of *Imagine*."

Soon everyone was gone and the four of us started walking down the trail back to the dinghy dock. Everything was quiet. No more commotion, no people running frantically around, just the four of us making our way home.

"You saved her life," I told my dad.

He stopped on the trail and replied, "No, Tommy, you and your dog saved her life."

My mom looked at my dad, leaned over, and—yep—kissed him right on the lips. I swear they had no respect for their children.

EIGHT

The next morning on *Imagine*, my mom and dad were busy looking at charts. They seemed to really enjoy plotting our next move. My dad's hands were bandaged from pulling on the rope the day before and he was ready for a couple of easy days.

The procedure was always the same. First we checked weather sources for wind and wave forecasts. Then we studied the *Pilot Guide*, a book that gives information for different places in the world regarding marine ports, typical weather patterns, currents, and a bunch of other stuff my dad seemed to think important.

The whole boat thing is a lot different from regular life stuff. I know I never looked at a *Pilot Guide* before heading off to summer camp. Those days were easy—just get in a car and go!

After looking everything over, my parents decided to spend one more night on our current mooring in the Bay of Eternity. This was fine with me and Caroline. After all, with all the lifesaving stuff we had been doing, we were ready for some regular exploring.

Just a few hundred yards from our boat was a large area of dry land—when the tide was out. When the tide was high, the water was over fifteen feet in the same spot. We wanted to hunt for clams while the place was dry. Not that either of us really liked clams, but the idea sounded fun. Our parents loved the things.

My dad gave us the green light, but before we could take off in the dinghy, he made us sit down at the chart table to look at the tide tables. This I found irritating. My dad already knew when the tide would be high and low, but he couldn't just tell us.

These so-called tables were impossible to understand. You had to look up your location from among hundreds listed in the tide tables, find the right date and time, and sometimes do math to figure out the time difference between where you were and where there was a tide-reporting station.

Caroline was all over it. She could do the math in seconds. I just nodded. I was sure I could do it faster than her, but I just wasn't interested. As soon as our dad was satisfied we had the times right, he turned us loose to explore.

I was second in the dinghy behind Rudder. Caroline jumped in with a collection bag over her shoulder. I pulled the cord on the outboard, put her in gear, and headed straight for the flats. Once we got there, we pulled the dinghy as far up on the mud as we could and walked the anchor forward another forty feet and stuck it in the mud.

Rudder was having a blast running around the huge open area of mud and sand. Finding clams was easy—they were everywhere. It was cool walking around knowing in that another six hours, our footprints would be covered by fifteen to twenty feet of water.

I was walking with my head down, looking for clams, and almost fell right over Rudder. As I caught my balance, I looked up and saw a huge bear only a few yards in front of me. I mean a real, live bear— teeth, claws, and everything. Caroline had no clue as she was still focused on the clam hunt.

"Ah, Caroline, don't move," I said as she approached me.

She froze. She saw the bear and stood motionless, as if she had turned to stone.

Rudder was just in front of us, his eyes focused hard on the bear. I was in panic mode. It seemed like a long time since a person or animal had moved. I was afraid for Rudder, as I knew he would go for the bear if we were challenged.

Finally, I slowly started backing up; Caroline did the same. We inched our way farther and farther as Rudder held his ground. I was sure this was going to be it for my best friend.

Caroline and I reached the dinghy anchor. I picked it up and we moved to the dinghy. It was easy to get it into the water now, as the tide had come up a couple of feet and the boat was almost floating. I pushed it back a bit and Caroline got in. I gave one more push and jumped in myself. I then yelled as loud as I could, "Come, Rudder, come."

He did not come. In fact, he moved slowly toward the bear. The hair on his back was raised and I could hear his low-pitched growl. The bear stood on his hind legs and made a sound like nothing I had ever heard. As Rudder stepped closer, the bear stepped back but looked as though he would attack at any moment.

I got out of the dingy and said to Caroline, "Stay in the boat. I'm going to get Rudder."

"No, Tommy. Don't be an idiot."

I could tell she was about to cry. I moved slowly, real slowly. I got closer to Rudder and softly said, "Rudder, come on, boy."

I repeated it a few times. Finally, he turned his attention away from the bear and looked at me. He took a couple of steps backward and the bear dropped down onto all fours. As Rudder and I crept backward, the bear seemed to relax. When we reached the dingy, I lifted Rudder in and then jumped in myself. The bear was slowly moving in the opposite direction.

When he was a safe distance away, I climbed back out of the dinghy and walked to the spot where we had met the bear.

Caroline screamed, "Tommy, now what are you doing?"

"Picking up the clam bag you dropped."

A few minutes later, the three of us were motoring back to *Imagine*, dinner in hand.

When we showed Mom and Dad our catch, we could see they were happy campers. My dad loves clams. Mom asked Caroline how the adventure went and she replied, "Fine, Mom. It was fun."

I was surprised until I realized she didn't want to tell our parents about the bear for fear that they might restrict us in the future. I hadn't thought of that. Sometimes the girl was pretty smart.

The next morning, we were back at sail, heading out of the Saquenay into the Gulf of St. Lawrence. Our goal was to head north and east to work our way toward Nova Scotia. This would take about a week to ten days with only a couple of marina options along the way. Usually, the plan each day was to find a cove to anchor in after getting some sailing miles under our belts.

As we pulled away from the bay, I couldn't help but think about how we had rescued that little girl. She will never know us—or us her. She will never really know her life goes on because of a peanut-butter-loving black dog. My dog.

NINE

The next morning, my dad gave me a break. He slipped the mooring (boat lingo for untied us) and sailed out into the river without starting the motor. It was nice not having to get up at five in the morning. By the time I woke up, my mom was already in the cockpit with my dad having coffee and blueberry muffins.

Rudder, as usual, was up on the bow like a lookout. I made two bowls of oatmeal, one with brown sugar for me and one regular for Rudder. I had heard someplace that oatmeal would help keep his cholesterol down, whatever that meant. Anyway, it was supposed to be a good thing and he loved it. A few hours later, we were out of the river and back into the open sea.

Almost all of the people around these parts were French Canadian—and I mean French. I never understood a single word. I couldn't figure out why they didn't speak English. I mean, America was just a little ways away, so how could they not speak the same language? The towns were all very small and there wasn't much in the way of roads, so I figured maybe they didn't get out far enough to learn a real language.

As we sailed *Imagine* day after day in the Gaspé, we often found ourselves in heavy fog—fog so thick that I couldn't see Rudder standing on the bow when I was in the cockpit. My dad stayed focused on the radar display. Sometimes we could hear a ship pass alongside but couldn't see it. My dad would just keep a plot of the ship on the radar and steer clear. It was hard to imagine how boats did it in the old days.

On about the third day after we left the Bay of Eternity, we were sailing in some bad fog in light wind, making only one knot. My mom and I were alone in the cockpit while my dad was taking a nap and Caroline was doing who knew what. I felt the boat move sideways a little bit, which boats like ours don't do. My mom and I looked at one another.

"Ah, Mom, did you feel that?"

"Yes, I felt that. What was it?"

"I don't know. Maybe we hit something," I answered.

We heard a loud sound right next to the boat. It was the clear noise of a whale blowing out water to take in its next breath. It was so close that the water it spouted rained down on us.

My mom and I froze, then both looked over the starboard side through the dense fog to see a humpback whale right up against the side of the boat. This whale was larger than *Imagine*! My dad had expressed concern about whales as there have been several cases of boats being sunk by them.

My mom slowly turned toward me and said, "Tommy, how about you quietly go below and wake your dad?"

I could see she was trying to be calm, but her face told another story.

My dad was quick on deck, but the whale was no longer in sight. On occasion, we could hear it blow not far away, but couldn't see it through the fog. This went on for about an hour. We slowly sailed toward our next stop, the Madeleine Islands—or, as the chart showed, Iles de la Madeleine.

My mom used times with calm seas and little wind for school catch-up. The islands were still over forty hours away, and, with the sea calm, we could sit comfortably at the dinner table and do our schoolwork. My program was a homeschool system called Calvert. I wasn't sure which one Caroline was following, but it wasn't the same as mine. I knew she had always been on some advanced program, but I had paid little attention to it.

My mom had been kind of a teacher before she quit her job for this little misadventure. I say "kind of a teacher" because I wasn't exactly sure what she did. People called her Doctor Tiller, but I knew she wasn't a regular doctor. She was a professor of physics at Northwestern University in Chicago. Much of her job involved doing research in energy systems, but she taught as well. She and Caroline often took separate time to do math and other meaningless school things, which I was happy not to be a part of. It was enough just getting through the endless lesson plans imposed on me for four hours a day, five days a week.

After finishing my school stuff, I was back on deck. The fog had cleared, the sun was out, and there wasn't a cloud in the sky. I had made a couple of peanut-butter-and-jelly sandwiches and gone up to the bow to hang out with Rudder. I had discovered he liked the strawberry jelly better than the grape. I had to agree.

I remember that day well. I wasn't sure why it seemed so special. It was just Rudder and me sitting on the bow of our little boat making tracks through the North Atlantic Ocean. We wouldn't see land until the next day. There were dolphins swimming just off the bow and I had gotten used to hearing whales spout. It somehow hit me that day just how cool I was.

My life had clearly changed. Not long ago, I was worrying about the chain coming off my bike. Now I worried about being struck by a fifty-foot whale! I used to worry about getting a hit in my baseball games, but now I was concerned with not falling overboard again.

Before we left, I was starting to get popular at school. I even kind of had a girlfriend. Now, I went days without even seeing another kid. I didn't count Caroline, not just because she was my sister, but also because she was more of an adult than our parents.

My life would never be the same again. As much as I did not want to be a part of this crazy adventure my parents had come up with, there I was. All the stuff I thought was so important back home no longer seemed to be.

Our next stop, after three and a half days of sailing, would be the remote Madeleine Islands, a place I had never heard of. Heck, I bet almost no one has heard of them, yet there we were, set to arrive in the morning. I was changing and I liked it.

That night conditions got rough. The wind and waves picked up dramatically and the boat was heeling hard. For about five hours, the wind blew at over thirty-three knots, which officially made it a gale.

A few months earlier, that would have freaked me out, but now it was just another day of dealing with trying to pee with the boat heeled over at thirty degrees. Around noon, the main Madeleine Island came into view. A few hours later, we were tied up to the end of a pier.

My dad gave Caroline and me twenty bucks and told us we could head out and find our own place for a late lunch. This was one of the cool things about the cruising lifestyle—us kids were often cut loose, which never happened in the normal world. So, with cash in hand and the green light from Mom and Dad, Caroline, Rudder, and I headed up the only road toward town.

We walked about a mile. We both knew our mom was going to like this place. There were several small, cool-looking art galleries and a restaurant with a sign out front advertising live classical piano at eight—both bonuses for our culture-starved mom.

Just as we were nearing the end of the road, we found a cool ice-cream shop with hot dogs that reminded us of the place on Beaver Island. This time, however, the floor wasn't moving under us. We had adjusted to moving from sea to land and back again pretty well.

We sat up at the soda bar and reviewed our options. It looked like our twenty was going to go a long way here. I ordered cheese fries with chili and a root beer for me and a hamburger for Rudder. Caroline ordered a salad and some fruit.

For some reason, she had decided about a month earlier to become a vegetarian. This made no sense to me, but trying to figure out why she did the stuff she did was impossible. She had watched a documentary called *Food, Inc.* and after that said she was done with any meat that wasn't free range—whatever the heck that meant.

About halfway through our meal, three kids close to my age came in and sat next to Caroline. They were creeps. They kept teasing Caroline for eating "rabbit food," but she was good at ignoring them. They spoke some English but mostly French. One of them even waved a hot dog in front of her face as if to dare her to eat it. I told him to knock it off, but they all just laughed at me. They probably didn't even know what I'd said.

When their bill came, Caroline said to the lady behind the counter, "Miss, you miscalculated their bill. It should be $21.50, not $11.50. You forgot to carry your one."

After a second look, the waitress quickly made the change. Caroline smiled at the boys. They did not smile back.

We left the soda shop and turned the corner to find the three creeps waiting for us. The biggest one came right up to me and pushed me up against a wall. In very broken English, he said, "What are you going to do about your little girlfriend?"

Or at least I thought that's what he said. I glanced at Rudder for a little help, but he just sat and watched. It was as if he had decided he wasn't needed for this situation. I disagreed.

Caroline looked at ease. She said to the kid, "C'est mon frère stupide."

I said, "What did you say? And how in the heck do you know how to speak French?"

The kid just ignored her and focused on me while his two buddies laughed. He shouted some more at me, but I couldn't understand. "Me no speak-ah no French-o," I said.

Just when I thought I was about to get pummeled, two more kids showed up. "Great," I thought, "now there are five of them to kill me.

To my great relief, however, one of the new kids said in perfect English, "Do you need some help here?"

Both of the new guys looked fit and fast; the three bad guys all looked a bit soft. The big guy let go of me. I didn't know who the new guys were, but they acted as though they knew who I was. We all stood there for a few minutes as if we were in an old Western movie showdown. I could tell that the French kids were sizing up the situation. Now it was three to three.

Finally, my new friend, the older of the two, said, "Well, boys, what's it going to be? My brother and I live on a boat so we're used to pain. Let's see what you've got."

I wasn't sure if the bullies understood English, but it became clear that they weren't going to fight. The one big guy said something to his friends and then yelled some things at Caroline in French. She answered back in French. Whatever she said really shut the kid up. They all walked away.

I was relieved. I turned to my two new best friends. "Thanks, you guys. My name is Tommy."

The older one replied, "Hi, I'm Grant, and this is my brother, Noah."

Turned out they were living full-time on their sailboat as well and were on the same crazy adventure as us. These were the first other kids I had met that shared the same kind of mentally unstable parents. Grant told us they were docked right next to our boat. My dad had told them where to find us. When you live on a boat, you're always looking for other kids.

"So what was it you said to that guy?" Noah asked Caroline.

"Oh, I told him I would love to stand here and engage in a battle of wits, but not with an unarmed boy."

Grant cracked up. It took me a moment to get it, but then we were all laughing. "My sister is a little odd," I explained.

Back at the dock, we had a blast. I could tell these guys had been doing this for a while. When we first got to their boat, Grant jumped from the dock to the bow. He grabbed the anchor and swung his feet up over the pulpit and onto the deck like a monkey in the trees. Noah ran down the dock and with one leap cleared the lifelines on their boat and landed clean on the aft deck. I could see that Caroline was impressed.

They invited Caroline and me onto their boat, a nice Hallberg-Rassy 46. Their dad, Marc, was on our boat helping my dad fix the generator. Their mom was very pretty. A real natural pretty. No makeup or fancy clothes, just a clean, happy look. Her name was Jane and she made Caroline and I feel very welcome. She had just made some oatmeal cookies and laid them out for the four of us kids to devour.

After the snack, we hit the water. Grant hoisted us up one at a time with a halyard to the first spreader on the mast. It was about twenty feet above the water and made a great jumping-off point. We made a few swan dives from the spreader and then snorkeled around the rocks for about an hour in search of lobsters. Although we didn't catch any, it was fun trying.

Later that night, the four adults went into town to the piano bar. The kids stayed on Grants' boat and played Monopoly for about four hours. It was crazy; Noah was a Monopoly master. By the time we finished, he owned just about the whole board.

We heard our parents coming down the dock at about two in the morning. They must have had a good time together. They were laughing at anything and everything. I guess the insane really hit it off with their own kind.

Both families stayed one more day and had a great time together. It was sad to think about saying goodbye. I found it very strange that I was going to miss my new friends more than I missed any of my old friends from school. It was kind of a natural bond. I had only known them for three days, yet it felt as though they had been friends my whole life.

On the day of departure, we exchanged contact information. It was really hard leaving our new friends. We were heading to Cape Breton Island in Nova Scotia and they were going to Newfoundland for a couple of weeks. The grown-ups talked about meeting up again in the Bras d'Or Lakes of Nova Scotia before heading down to Halifax. We helped each other untie the boats and then sailed together for about three hours until our slightly different courses took us out of sight of one another.

Once we started heading south, they disappeared over the horizon. "I guess it's just you and me again," I said to Rudder. "Oh, and by the way, buster, where was the help back with those thugs?"

Caroline piped up, "Oh, Tommy, give him a break. Rudder knew you could have taken that guy with one arm tied behind your back."

I thought, "Of course, no wonder he didn't seem concerned at the soda shop. He's smart enough to know I had the whole situation under control."

After we settled into our normal routine of passage-making—sailing long out of sight of land—I decided to go have a little talk with my mom.

"Okay, Mom, what's the deal with Caroline?"

"What do you mean?"

"Mom, the girl speaks French. She doesn't do schoolwork with me. It's just the two of you all the time. She can do any math in her head, and again, she speaks French! What's the deal?"

"Well, come on, Tommy, you know that Caroline is very advanced with school."

"Well, yeah, I know she's good at math and does advanced school stuff, but come on, French?"

My mom paused for a moment and said, "Well, Caroline is special when it comes to learning."

"What do you mean, 'special'? Like how special? What grade is she actually in?"

It was as though my mom didn't really want to tell me. Finally, she said, "Caroline is not in a grade."

What the heck was that supposed to mean?

She went on, "She can't really be placed into a grade. She does advanced college math and theory, but her social studies is only at about eleventh- or twelfth-grade level."

"Eleventh grade! But, Mom, she's only ten! And what about the speaking French thing? What's with that?"

"I don't know. She just reads and learns faster than most. She can speak a little Spanish, too."

I felt pretty dumb at that moment. I knew we had moved to Chicago to put her in a school for gifted children, and I knew she could do my math problems in her head without even thinking. She talked more grown-up than the grown-ups and she always seemed to have trouble making friends her own age. The more I thought about it, I realized that as far back as I could remember, she'd been different.

"But, Mom, why didn't we ever have one of those 'family meetings' you and dad are so fond of to discuss this?"

"Remember, Tommy, she is only ten. Emotionally she is just that—ten. Your dad and I have always tried to keep things as normal as possible for her. We try not to make a big deal about it but at the same time allow her to grow academically."

"So is she a genius?"

"We don't really care for that term," she replied

"Well, is she?"

"Okay, yes. She is genius."

Perhaps I'd always known it, but somehow it still seemed like news. I asked,

"Like a little genius or a lot genius?"

I could tell that my mom didn't really want to talk too much about it, but she knew the time had come to be up front with me. She answered, "Caroline has an almost off-scale IQ. She is more advanced in mathematics than most college math professors. She can read a page of normal text in about two seconds and recall everything from the page. She is also fluent in almost all computer languages, including older formats like Fortran. She can write in C, C++, Small talk, Hyper-Talk, and on and on. She can also write cross-platform, such as to Mac, Windows, and Sun. It doesn't matter—they all come natural to her. Even the way she can play the piano is because to her, the keys are nothing but numbers that all make sense."

After my mom's explanation, there was a rather long pause. She sat patiently with me in case I had more questions. I had none. I had always known that Caroline was a little weird, but holy smokes, that kind of confirmation took a bit of getting used to. Before we parted, my mom added, "Now, Tommy, please respect that for Caroline, this is all normal. Don't make her feel out of place and for sure do not discuss it with others, as it only ends up making her an outcast."

I understood what my mom was saying and would respect her request. Caroline was a pain, but I wouldn't do anything to hurt her.

Later that night in the cockpit, I asked my dad, "Dad, you always knew about Caroline?"

"What do you mean?" he replied.

"About her being really smart and all."

"Well, sure, Tommy," he said. "I mean, it was pretty obvious from the get-go. Didn't you wonder why she went with Mom to the university every day instead of to regular school?"

I realized I'd never really given it much thought. It made me realize that there were a lot of things I never gave much thought to. It was perhaps at that moment that I came to understand that in order to see, you had to look.

"Well, if we have the same parents, shouldn't I be just as smart?" I asked.

My dad chucked a bit and answered, "We all have different kinds of intelligence. Caroline is something of a math prodigy and her mind can absorb information very fast. There are things you can do and see better than her, however. Just different things."

I sat for a moment and wondered if I wanted to pursue my dad's comment, but pushed on, "So when you say 'different,' what do you mean?"

"Remember the night we were anchored in Tadoussac and the wind came up at gale strength?"

"Yes," I replied.

"The wind was causing our anchor to drag and was sending us closer to shore. I called you up on deck and you looked around and said, 'Dad, we'd better pull anchor and get out of here.' Remember?"

I nodded.

"Well, son, had I called Caroline up, or your mom, for that matter, neither would have had a quick action plan. They could both tell us at our current rate of drag exactly how long before we hit shore, but neither would be on top of an exit plan. You have a brilliant action mind. They make generals out of brains like yours."

That was all I needed to hear. It was as if the earth was somehow rotating on its proper axis again. "Did you hear that, boy?" I said to Rudder. "Not only am I tough, but I also have the stuff of generals!"

Rudder tilted his head to one side. I swear that if he could speak, he would have said, "*Whate*ver." It didn't matter. I knew he understood.

TEN

The sail from Iles de la Madeleine to Cape Breton Island in Nova Scotia was only about twelve hours. The seas were big, with waves of about sixteen feet. The sea conditions were bad because there was almost no wind and we were motoring through big seas left-over from a storm in Newfoundland a few days earlier. Normally, waves are associated with strong wind. At least when it's blowing, the sails heel the boat to one side and it does not roll back and forth. With no wind and thus no sail, we rolled horribly. After a while, it really makes you feel sick. I was tired of rolling and motoring and ready for a protected harbor. Unfortunately, motoring on a sailboat like ours only makes about six to seven knots. With sixty miles to go, even I could figure out that we were looking at another ten hours or so.

Finally, late in the day my dad turned the boat to starboard and headed toward land. I was pretty happy to be heading in, but saw no harbor or opening and asked, "Ah, Dad, you do see there is land in front of us, right?"

He paid no attention to me. He was focused on the chart plotter and radar. When we got to about one mile from shore and there was still no harbor in sight, I said, "Hate to be a pest here, Dad, but we should be crashing into shore in about eight minutes."

My dad replied, "Relax, Tommy. We're heading into a small fishing village called Dingwall."

"But there's no opening," I protested.

Imagine stayed on course, pointing straight at nothing but rocks and uninhabited shore. When we got about a quarter-mile from an almost certain crash, I could see two small buoys, one red, on the right, and the other green, to our left. At this point, I had to assume there was an entrance.

The big seas lifted the stern of *Imagine* up high and caused her bow to lower and push thirty or forty degrees one way or the other. My dad was all over the wheel. He would turn the helm hard one way, then equally as hard the other. Soon, we were centered between the two channel markers with only about two feet separating either of them from our hull.

What I thought was a continuous shore turned out to have a small opening about twenty-five feet across. My dad fought the waves right into the opening and soon, by some miracle, we were safely inside a small fishing harbor.

There were six good-sized fishing boats with nets and gear, but from what I could see, only about five houses along the shore. It was as though there were more fishing boats than people.

We anchored in the middle of the bay as it was small and the boat needed room to swing around when the wind changed. My dad put the dinghy in the water and motored over to one of the trawlers.

When he got back, he said, "The locals say we are okay to stay anchored here, but we will hear them leaving in the morning about four-thirty."

"Wow, some guys are crazier than my dad," I thought.

After getting all the normal arrival chores done, I climbed in the dinghy with Rudder and headed to town. We tied up to an old dock that was pretty much falling apart. Rudder jumped to land and I quickly followed.

We walked up toward a dirt road and ran into a woman working in her garden. I figured it was her dock, so I asked, "Miss, is it okay that we tied our dinghy to your dock?"

"Sure, but be careful. It has a lot of broken boards," she replied.

First, I was glad she spoke English, since without Caroline to translate I would have been back to communicating with my own kind of sign language. "Boy, it's nice you can speak English," I said.

"Well, of course, boy, this is Canada, not Spain."

I was thinking she meant *not France,* like the place many of her Canadian neighbors think they live. Anyway, it was nice to be back in a normal language place. "Where is the town?" I asked.

"You're standing in pretty much downtown," she said and laughed. "If you're looking for a store, you will have to walk about a half-mile that way." She pointed up the road.

"Thanks," I replied, and Rudder and I took off up the road.

Just like the lady said, about a half-mile up the road we found a store, a church, and a bar. It seemed like no matter how small any town was, it always had a store, a church, and a bar.

I went into the little store and bought a Butterfinger for me and a blueberry muffin for Rudder. I figured he shouldn't eat candy, given that he never brushed his teeth.

When I came out of the store, I noticed a large, castle-looking place high in the hills. When we got back to the lady working in her garden, I asked, "What's that big place way up in the hills?"

She replied, "You don't want to know. Just leave that be."

Well, I didn't know if she had kids, but to tell a guy my age "just leave that be" has little chance of working. "Well, does anyone live there?" I asked.

"No one has lived there for years. The house is too dangerous and unstable. Much of the mountain has collapsed next to it and before long the whole house will fall off that ledge. Don't go up there. No one goes there."

"Come on," I replied. "You're telling me no one goes up there, not even kids on a dare?"

"They have tried in the past, but there is no way to get there."

"How do you know no one lives there?"

"My, you ask a lot of questions, young man. An old man, a scientist they say, built the place many years ago. He lived there but he's been gone for over twenty years."

I just wasn't buying that in all those years, no one had gone up to explore. I needed more information, so I turned around and headed back up the road to the store we had just left. I went inside and asked the guy behind the counter, "Hey, mister, who lives in that house up there?" I pointed up the hill.

He acted as if he hadn't heard me, so I asked again.

"No one lives up there," he answered. "It's just a run-down house with snakes and danger. You don't want to go there. Besides, there's no safe way to get there. In fact, there really isn't *any* way to get there."

"Seriously?" I replied.

He looked at me kind of sternly and said, "Listen, kid, I'm telling you, it's not safe up there. Think of it as off-limits. Besides, like I said, there is nothing there but snakes and rubble."

I just couldn't give up yet. "Well, how did they build it if you can't get there?" I asked.

"Years ago, there was a small road, but over time it became overgrown and filled with boulders that fell from higher up. A ledge eventually gave way and created the sheer cliff with no way up or down. That's how we know no one lives there. An old man used to live there, but he's been gone for years. No one has been up or down for over twenty-five years."

I looked up at the house again as I left the store. It was as if it was calling to me. It looked almost as though there was a mist around it. I had never seen anything like it.

Rudder and I went back to the dock and climbed in the dinghy. The lady in the garden was gone. I started the outboard and headed to *Imagine.*

My dad was busy fixing a bad shower pump and Caroline and my mom were doing math. Sometimes the boat could be really boring. I climbed into my bunk to read a little but couldn't stop thinking about the house. I left my bunk and asked my dad, "So, Dad, how long do we plan to stay here?"

"I think we'll stay a few days and let the weather settle."

I went out on deck. I could see the house from the boat. I looked through the binoculars and could see a big, dark, broken-down mansion. It had two turrets, like a castle. And just as the guy in the store had said, there appeared to be no road or path to the place.

I needed a better look, so I got my mom's camera with the big telephoto lens. It was two to three times more powerful than the binoculars. I zoomed in, but no matter what I did, the house wouldn't come into focus. I tried auto focus and manual, but had no luck.

I finally fetched my mom and asked her to help. She and Caroline were pretty much done with their math playtime. She came on deck, looked up at the house, and said, "My, that is out there by itself, isn't it?"

She grabbed the camera and made some adjustments but didn't snap any shots.

"Odd," she said.

"What do you mean?" I asked.

"I can't seem to focus," she replied.

"I know, that's what I have been saying. Is something wrong with your camera?"

My mom aimed at other spots and said, "No, the camera is functioning fine."

"So what's the problem then?"

"I'm not sure, Tommy. There seems to be some kind of atmospheric interference."

Normally I would have kept asking questions, but I decided to drop it. Perhaps the lady in the garden had been right to tell me to let it be.

That night was pretty normal other than the wind blowing extra hard through the rigging. I finished dinner, did my schoolwork, and went to bed. When I tried to sleep, I couldn't get my mind off the abandoned house.

"Let it be?"

"Yeah, right," I thought, "like that could happen."

ELEVEN

I got up early. It was about eight and my dad was on the phone arranging to get a ride to a bigger town to get a part for the shower pump. Caroline had made some French toast with granola baked on top. I was impressed and hungry.

After breakfast, I asked my dad if I could ride to the shore with him so I could explore some. "Sure, Tommy," he said, "but I will be gone for several hours, so how do you plan to get back to the boat?"

"I will swim back or just wait by the dinghy for you," I replied.

My dad was fine with that and we prepared to take off. I packed my backpack with two peanut-butter-and-jelly sandwiches, a flashlight, and the portable VHF radio so I could call back to *Imagine* if needed.

When we got to shore, my dad hooked up with the ride he had arranged and took off. Rudder and I headed toward the house. I kept hearing that lady's words in my head: "Just let it be."

"That was lame," I thought. After all, it was just a house. The idea of the place being haunted didn't bother me much. I was sure there was no such thing.

Besides, it wasn't like I had a lot of other things to do that day.

The first hard part was finding a way up. I walked back and forth for a while, traversing the hill. The woods were dense and the terrain was really steep, so making headway was difficult. After a couple of hours, I was frustrated at having made almost no real headway toward the house. It looked as if there really was no way up.

About the time I was ready to give up, I noticed what looked like an old path. It was hard to tell if it was actually a path, but Rudder seemed to want to follow it. I stayed close to him. I was impressed that Rudder could make his way over large boulders. He looked part billy goat.

We weaved back and forth and continued up and up. I got nervous about finding our way back down and knew it was easier going up than down. The trees and brush made it impossible to see far enough ahead to get my bearings. I couldn't even see the harbor.

After about another half an hour, or about three hours into our journey, we came to an end. That was fine. I figured we should head back at that point, anyway. I was ready to give up when Rudder disappeared into the rocks. I followed, and to my amazement, there was a small but defined tunnel. Iron bars had blocked the entrance at some point but time had taken care of them and they were now rusted out. I could only see about ten feet with the help of my flashlight, but the tunnel was large enough that if stooped over, I could go in.

I had no idea if it would lead to anywhere. I was kind of hoping it would lead to an easier way down, to be honest. Rudder had gone ahead and I decided to follow. The tunnel was small, but I could walk along it if I kept bent over. After only about twenty feet, it was so dark I couldn't see my hand in front of my face. I kept my flashlight focused forward. Rudder stayed just inches in front of me as we moved farther into the tunnel.

Clearly, this was a man-made tunnel. We came across steep areas that had steps carved out of the rock to make going up just like going up any set of stairs, only bent over. Rudder was lucky; he walked on all fours as per normal while I was stooped over like a hunchback.

Rudder suddenly stopped after about thirty minutes of climbing. I bumped right into his rear end and said, "Come on, Rudder, keep moving."

He took another step but stopped again. He held his position. I shined the light up in front of him and could see nothing, but as I did I felt something on my foot.

I pointed the flashlight down and, to my horror, there was a large black snake moving over my foot. I froze. I knew it was time to turn around.

After the snake moved off my foot, I turned to head back out the way we came. I shined the light the direction we had come in and froze again. The whole floor was covered with black snakes. There were so many that I couldn't even see the floor anymore.

I looked toward Rudder. There were some snakes where he was but only a few—nothing like what was now behind us. There was no choice but to keep moving forward.

I nudged Rudder. He took a couple of steps at a time, moving very slowly. I shuffled along, too, afraid I would step on a snake.

We inched along and I was flat-out scared. Now and then, I would hear the hiss from right next to me. I kept the flashlight facing forward, trying to avoid looking at the ground.

I could only see Rudder if I shined the light directly on him, so I tried to keep some physical contact as we crept along. With my hand on his upper rear, I felt something. Rudder stopped. I pointed the light downward to see two big snakes moving on his back. One had just passed over my hand. At first, they were hard to see against his black body, but they were really there. Rudder stood still and patient.

When I shined the light at the snakes, they seemed bothered by it. I suppose they didn't normally see light. It was enough bother that they slithered off Rudder and back into the crevasses of the floor.

I kept waiting for the pain of a bite. I just wanted to run as fast as I could out of there but I couldn't stand up straight and would be running over a floor of snakes.

It took everything in me to keep my cool. I was amazed at how methodical Rudder was. Since the light seemed to cause the snakes to move away, I kept shining it on the floor in front of us. Each time Rudder stepped, I stepped. I started wondering how old the batteries were. The thought of no light was terrifying, so I tried to stay focused.

Rudder stopped again. I tried to nudge him forward until I realized there was no forward. We had reached the end of the tunnel. It looked as if there was no way to go except back the way we had come. The idea of that was something I wasn't sure I could face. I shined the light all the way around but didn't see an exit. I knelt down for a moment, put my hand on Rudder's head, and said, "Boy, I think we're going to die here."

I set the light down to give Rudder a pat with both hands. When I went to pick it back up, I noticed it was shining on a piece of wood. As I looked more closely, I could see that it was a ladder going straight up along the far corner of the cave.

I shined the flashlight up, but it was too far to see. The light just shined into empty darkness. The ladder seemed to be the only option, but I didn't know what to do with Rudder. I assumed dogs couldn't climb ladders.

As we stood there, I felt something on my leg. Not just on my leg, but crawling up the inside of my pants. This was not possible. A snake was making its way up the bare skin of my leg. If I thought I was panicked before, it was nothing compared to that moment. I was still hunched over and now frozen like a piece of concrete. The snake didn't seem able to make the turn at the bend of my knee, but it wasn't heading south, either. I could feel it tighten around my leg a bit and then relax and move just a little bit more. It would start heading back up my leg, get stuck at the bend, and then repeat the process. It felt almost like liquid going up my leg. I moved the flashlight to have a look at it. It was huge and as black as the darkness. Part of it was still on the floor and the rest was halfway up my leg. I was as scared as a person could be.

Rudder started to move a little. I whispered, "Rudder, stay. Don't move, boy."

We both stood there for what seemed like forever. Finally, the snake worked its way back down to the floor and out of my pants. I was trembling and felt unable to move, but at that point I knew that some-how, someway, we were going up that ladder.

I reached down, put both my hands under Rudder's chest, and lifted his front legs up to the third rung of the ladder. He seemed to know what to do right away and started to pull himself up. He was actually good at it. I kept a hand on his rear end and pushed him along as we climbed.

The ladder was about three feet short at the top, so I pushed Rudder up and over the edge. I reached up, set the flashlight on the ledge, and placed my hands over it. I was so afraid that there would be snakes where I put my hands. Once I got a good enough grip over the top, I pulled myself up, expect-ing to be greeted by the same horror as below.

I sat there for a few moments and scanned with the flashlight. No snakes anywhere. I was so relieved. I felt like I could start breathing again. The new tun-nel wasn't very tall either, so I still had to stay hunched over, but I was used to it by now.

There was only one way to go, as far as I could tell. Rudder moved much faster. It felt good to be making better time now, but, within just a few feet, I felt something on my neck. I knelt down, reached behind my neck, and knocked something off.

I looked up at the roof with the flashlight and almost flipped out. The entire ceiling was covered with bats. I mean *covered*. There was no exposed rock, only bats—thousands of them. I wanted to turn around and get out of there. I was again in panic mode. I didn't really know anything about bats. In fact, I had never seen one before, but for some rea-son, I was again scared out of my wits. I felt there was no way I could keep going, but even if I could get

Rudder down the ladder some fifty feet, there were the snakes to contend with. I was consumed with fear. Then Rudder came up next to me, licked my face, and started to move forward. He kept looking back at me to make sure I was coming. As I got up the courage to follow, I started to feel more and more in control. It was nice knowing Rudder was calm and in front.

Then it hit me. First, if we ever did find the house, how would we get back down? Second, even if we didn't find the house, how would we get back down? I knew I had messed up this time. Sure enough, those words kept coming back: "Just let it be."

Since it appeared that there were no more snakes, I decided to crawl on all fours like Rudder. This kept me farther from the bats. The only problem was holding the light, so I ended up kind of crawling on one arm and two legs with the light still on and in my right hand. I was trying to stay as far away from the ceiling as possible.

The floor was wet and smelly. I knew it was from the bats, but there was nothing I could do. We just kept moving, slowly but surely, making much better time than we had when we were down with the snakes. I believed that if I survived this day, I would never leave the boat again.

After about fifteen minutes, the wet smelly stuff was gone. I pointed the light up and saw nothing. Not just no bats, but no anything. No ceiling, no walls—just a big empty space. I thought maybe we had entered a big cave, but then I noticed that the floor was wood, not rock.

We moved slowly, looking for anything, but my light was starting to fade. Sure enough, the batteries were dying. At least I could stand up now. We walked several feet in each direction, but never found a wall. Whatever this room was, it was big.

Finally, my light went out and we were in total darkness. I could feel Rudder at my side but could see nothing. Then Rudder started to growl. He knew there was someone or something in the room with us. I stood in horror, stuck to the floor as if glued.

Rudder was getting restless. We just stood there in the emptiness. I could feel his tension. Out of nowhere came the voice of a woman. "Who are you and how did you get here?"

I was freaked. I couldn't tell where the voice was coming from. It seemed to be all around us. Rudder began to growl with more strength and the woman said, "Dog, you will calm now."

Rudder was suddenly silent. She again asked, "Who are you?"

I said, "I'm Tommy Tiller, and next to me is my dog, Rudder."

"How did you get into this room?" she asked.

"We came through the tunnel."

In a much louder voice, she replied, "Don't lie to me, boy. No one can come through the tunnel. The snakes in there are deadly and no one could make it through, let alone a boy and a dog."

I couldn't believe what I was hearing. Had I known for sure that the snakes were deadly when I was down there, I would have had a heart attack.

"We walked through the black snakes, both of us, and then we went up a ladder to the tunnel with the bats."

The room was silent. The woman did not speak. The darkness was overwhelming and I had no idea what to do.

"Are you still here?" I asked.

Still nothing. I tried a couple more times, but only the dark silence answered me. Rudder had moved away from my side. Once I could no longer feel him, I had no idea where he was. I called, "Rudder, Rudder, come, boy, come."

Normally, he would be right there, but this time he didn't come. I stayed frozen in my position, blind and suddenly alone.

Then I felt something against the back of my leg. I stayed still and silent. Something touched my hand; it was Rudder. I was about to lose my mind.

After about five minutes, a small ray of light appeared by a ladder in the corner of the room. I moved quickly to the light with Rudder right next to me. We went up the ladder and found a door that opened into a regular room, a room that actually had high windows and light. I couldn't remember ever being more happy to be out of a place than I was at that moment.

We moved across the room to another door, which opened into a long hallway. I could tell we were in the house. It had yet to occur to me it was *the* house.

I looked down the length of the hall and started walking. Every few feet, I said, "Miss, are you there? We are sorry."

Finally, we entered a large room with a huge fireplace. Beautiful furniture and large paintings were on the walls. We walked a few feet in and I could see the woman sitting in a large chair with her back to us. "Sit down, boy," she said.

I did.

"That dog is special, you know?"

"Yes, I know," I replied. "He saved my life in the St. Lawrence River."

"No," the woman said. "He is different. There is something very special in him."

I didn't know what to say. I just sat there like the dummy Caroline often referred to me as.

"Why are you here?" the woman asked. She sounded kind of scared.

"Well, I was told the house was haunted. I didn't believe it. I was also told that no one lived here. I just wanted to see for myself."

The woman seemed to be crying. "Ah, are you okay, lady?"

She didn't reply. I waited, and after another few minutes, I asked again, "Are you okay? Are you alone here?"

She answered, "I am alone. I have been alone for a very long time." She paused for a while and then added, "How can it be that after all these years, it is a little boy that finds me here?"

"Well, I'm really not that little. I will be thirteen pretty soon. But what do you mean about finding you?"

She continued to cry. "I have been alone in this house since my grandfather died."

"How long ago was that?" I asked.

"I was seven when he died. He died right here in this room."

That gave me the creeps. I looked around for a minute, wondering just where in the room he'd died. I asked, "Well, after his funeral, why didn't you go and stay with your family?"

After wiping her eyes, she answered softly, "There was no funeral. He died here. I put him in the cellar downstairs. He's still there."

Now I was thinking I had entered the twilight zone. This could not be true. Was I to believe there was a dead guy in the cellar? I was also wondering how far away the cellar was. I didn't know what to think at that point. "Why didn't you call someone to come and help you?"

"You don't understand," she said. "There is no help. This house has no electricity, no lights—not even candles anymore. No phone and no way to get out."

This was nuts—or *she* was nuts. What she was saying could not be true.

"If you can't get out, then how do you get food and stuff?"

She calmly replied, "There is enough food here to last several lifetimes. My grandfather built a food storage room downstairs. Most things you only have to add water to eat. Water flows year round from the mountain and the heat comes from something my grandfather built in the earth."

"But there has to be a way back down to the town other than the tunnel."

She turned to face me, tears in her eyes. I couldn't tell how old she was, but she didn't look much older than my mom.

"My grandfather took me in after my parents were killed in a plane crash. He lived and worked here, but was afraid people would steal his ideas. He built the tunnels and brought in the snakes to guard against intruders. There was only one way in or out besides the tunnel, and that disappeared when part of the mountain collapsed in front of the house just before he died."

"So are you saying that the only way down is through the tunnel that I came up?"

"Yes," she said. "I have tried. I have searched for years for a way down, but the cliffs are just too steep and tall. I don't even have rope."

"How was your grandfather ever going to get down?"

"I don't know, but he said he had a way."

"But why has no one come for you?" I asked.

"No one knows I'm here."

"Couldn't you try to signal someone or something?"

"I have tried everything over the years," she explained. "I even tried a mirror to get attention, but the light just reflects back at me. I think it might have something to do with the energy system my grandfather built. I finally gave up." After a pause she asked, "Does anyone know you're here?"

I thought about it and realized the answer was no, but... I reached into my backpack and pulled out the portable VHF radio from *Imagine*. "I can call for help with this radio. My parents will be listening once they realize I'm not back on the boat."

The woman started to cry. She reached to me and said, "So you can take me away from here?"

"Sure, I'll just get on the radio and call my mom and dad."

She looked unsure of what to do. I figured she would be excited, but she sat back down and said, "I'm not sure I can go."

"Why not?" I asked. "Don't you want to get out of here?"

"I'm sorry, but I'm really afraid. I don't think I can do it."

I sat next to her, put her hand on Rudder's head, and said, "Trust the black dog. You already know he's special. If he can walk me though the tunnel of snakes, he can walk you back to the human race."

She seemed okay. She looked at Rudder and then back at me. With just one tear on her cheek, she said, "Okay, Tommy. Please call for help. But please, please don't tell anyone else. I'm afraid."

TWELVE

I turned on the VHF radio and dialed in channel 71, the channel we had agreed to always use. I made several attempts, but all I could hear was static. I tried all over the house to get a signal but to no avail. This was strange, because the boat was only about two or three miles away. Then I remembered my mom and the camera. She had said there was atmospheric disturbance or something.

"How can I get outside?" I asked the lady.

"Outside of this room?"

"No," I replied. "How do I get outside the house so I can use the radio? There must be a door."

She looked almost confused. "The only door is in the cellar, but that opens directly over the cliff and there is no deck or anything. It's been like that since the mountain collapsed. The rest of the house is built into the mountain."

I thought about going to the door and opening it just to see if I could get a signal. The problem was that according to the woman, there was a dead guy in the cellar and I wasn't too keen on finding him. I looked everywhere for an escape. The only thing I could think of was to try and get on the roof of one of the two turrets. There was a window that let in light that would allow access to the roof, but I had to figure out how to get up there.

I put the radio in the backpack. After stacking several chairs on a table, I was able to climb up to one of the windows. There was no way to open it, so I used the back end of my flashlight to break the glass.

After getting rid of all the sharp edges, I pulled myself up onto the roof. From there, I could actually see *Imagine*. The dinghy was tied to the back, so I knew my dad was back. The only problem with being on the roof was the fact that it was so steep. I could barely hold on with both hands and I needed at least one for the radio. I spread my legs and used the balls of my feet as best I could. I released one hand and slowly reached around for my backpack. I knew that with one false move I would fall about three hundred feet. I managed to get the radio, but as I pulled it out I lost grip on the backpack and could do nothing but watch it fall out of sight.

I got on the radio. "*Imagine, Imagine, Imagine*, this is Tommy on 71."

I tried it a few times, but was getting no reply. I was about to give up when the radio came to life with my mom's voice, "Tommy, this is *Imagine*, do you copy?"

"Yes, I copy," I replied.

"Tommy, where are you?"

"I am up at the house high up on the cliff. Do you copy?"

My mom answered, "Yes, I hear you, but there is a lot of static. Do you mean the house we tried to look at with the camera?"

"Yes, and I'm afraid I'm going to need some help to get down from here."

It was hard to hear because of the static, but after several transmissions, it was clear that my parents wanted more details. I filled her in on as much as I could but was trying to get her to figure out a way to get me down.

"Mom, listen carefully," I said. "If you find a tunnel leading up, do not—I repeat, do not—go into the tunnel. It is very dangerous. You must find another way up."

The radio was silent for a couple of minutes and then my dad came on. I could tell he was mad.

"What are you talking about, Tommy?"

"Dad, there is a tunnel, but it's filled with dangerous snakes. You can't come up that way, and I can't go down that way."

There was another pause, this one longer. I could only guess how confused my parents must have been. Finally, my dad came back on and said, "We will talk with the locals and find out how to get there."

For some reason, the lady was afraid of anyone knowing about her. She had begged me to talk only to my parents. I knew it would not be easy, but somehow I had to convince my dad to go it alone. I was trying to be careful because anyone could be listening on channel 71.

Then I remembered the get-out-of-jail-free card he had given me. That card meant that if I got myself into trouble, I could call and get picked up with no questions asked. I think my dad intended it for if I ended up at someone's house and they were drinking or something, but he had been clear—one free pass with no questions.

I got back on the radio and said, "Dad, I want to cash in my get-out-of-jail-free card. Do you understand?"

The radio was quiet again for what seemed like forever. Then my dad called back, "Is there something you're not telling us"?

"Dad, please trust me. If you can think of a way to get me out of here without a bunch of people, it would be better. And remember, if you find a tunnel, do not go in. Do you copy"?

"I copy. Stand by."

I was hoping I wouldn't be standing by for long, as my feet and left hand were getting pretty tired. Then I heard my father's voice again. "Okay, Tommy, we have a plan. Now listen up—your mother will climb to you with rope and gear. Do not leave. Do you understand?"

"Yes," I said.

"This will take some time. Are you hurt?"

"No, I am not hurt. Rudder is with me and we are fine, but there is no way down. If Mom is coming up the face, there is a door with no deck. I know none of this makes sense, but trust me, it will"

My dad's final words were, "Just sit there and wait, and you better hope you never need to get out of jail."

I knew I was in trouble—nothing new for me. I also knew that when they learned the rest of the story, they would forget the part about me being in trouble.

I decided to stay on the roof as long as I could so the radio would work if either of my parents tried to call back. Once I saw my parents get in the dingy, I worked my way back into the house, which was actually harder than getting out. Inside, I found the lady still sitting in the same chair. "My mom is going to climb up with rope and gear. She should be here in a couple of hours."

I was glad it stayed light until almost ten o'clock at that time of year.

The lady was worried and sad. "The cliffs are too steep. She cannot climb up here. It's not possible."

"You will be surprised. My mom will be here before you know it."

Unbeknownst to the lady, my mom was from Colorado and was an expert free rock climber. When I was a little kid, I often watched her climb straight up sheer mountain faces without a single rope. She loved it. I was sure she would still be doing it if my dad hadn't convinced her to give it up after a fall and a broken leg.

I couldn't believe what had happened. Could it really be true this woman had been in the house alone all those years? With some terror, I thought back to how Rudder and I had made our way through the snakes. I figured I might never go in another cave or tunnel again for the rest of my life. Just the thought of being back in that tunnel made me shiver.

I climbed back up to the window and perched myself on the roof. I keyed in the radio and called, "*Imagine, Imagine,* Tommy here."

"*Imagine* here."

"Tommy here looking for an update."

My mom's familiar voice came back, "I am starting my ascent now. Caroline and Dad will stay at the bottom."

"Be careful, Mom," I replied. "It's a long way up."

I heard her say in a muffled voice, "You can say that again."

It took my mom almost three hours to climb the cliff face—longer than I thought. When she finally got to the top, I heard her actual voice. "Tommy, can you hear me?"

I shouted back, "I hear you, Mom."

"There is a big door in the front of the house at the top of the cliff. You have to open it for me to climb up and in."

I shouted back, "But there is a dead guy in that room."

It was quiet for a few seconds, and then my mom said, "Tommy, you must open that door. I have no option here."

I was scared to go in the cellar but had no choice. "Okay, I'm on it."

I crawled back through the broken window, lowered myself to the chairs, and worked my way to the floor.

"How do I get into the cellar?" I asked the lady.

"It is dark down there and we have no light. Also, I told you my grandfather is down there."

There was nothing I could do.

"Look, my mom is hanging on just outside that door. Now how do I get in?"

She got up and walked me through a hallway and down some steps. Then she opened a door. "This is it," she said.

I started down the stairs into the cellar. The light coming in from the windows up in the hallway helped for the first half, but then it got really dark. Rudder was with me and, as usual, I tried to follow him.

The stairs seemed to go on forever, and then before I knew it I tripped over something and fell down the last ten or fifteen stairs. I hurt my wrist but was okay overall.

Rudder and I walked in all directions, feeling along the walls in search of a doorknob or latch. Finally, I felt what was surely a wooden bar over a latch and opened it. The two big doors flung open, letting in precious light. I was so happy. I noticed right away that there was no space between the doors and the cliff, just a straight drop-off.

My mom's head popped up and she pulled herself into the room. I thought I was really going to get an earful, but she said, "You ready to get out of here?"

I was relieved she wasn't yelling at me, but then I had to tell her, "Ah, Mom, there is a woman upstairs who says she has been alone here since she was seven. She wants out."

My mom looked stunned. "What did you just say?"

"I said there is a woman who has been trapped in this house for years. She wants out and I told her you could help."

"Let's go, Tommy," she said. "Show me this woman. Any other surprises you want to tell me about?"

"Not at the moment."

She gave me that look that only a mom can give, but then started toward the stairs.

With light from the open door and a new flashlight, it was easy to find our way back to the stairs. We started up and my mom screamed, "Shi...!"

I don't think I had ever heard her swear before. "I told you there was a dead guy in this room," I said.

It was now obvious what I'd tripped over. The remains of the grandfather were right on the steps. He still had his clothes on but there was nothing but bone. My mom was a little freaked, but she stepped over the body and went up the stairs with me, Rudder right behind us.

I led my mother to the great room, and the lady was sitting there, crying again. My mom went right up and sat next to her. "My name is Donna. What's yours?"

She waited a few seconds before replying, "My name is Susan. Susan Benson."

My mom said, "Well, Susan, it seems we have a lot to talk about."

Susan didn't say anything. My mom looked around the room and suddenly stood up as if she'd seen a ghost. Pointing to a large painting on the wall, she said, "Is that Carl Benson?"

Susan answered, "Yes, that's my grandfather."

My mom had to sit down. She kept staring at the portrait. "Tommy, do you know who Carl Benson is?"

"I guess he's the dead guy in the cellar," I replied.

"That man may have been the greatest scientist of our time," my mom said. "A pioneer in thermodynamics and particle physics."

To Susan, she said, "I met your grandfather when I was accepted to undergraduate school at MIT in Boston. I was only sixteen at the time, but I remember him well. He sponsored my acceptance at MIT."

"Sixteen at MIT?" I thought. Well, that explained a few things.

My mom went on, "The year I got to Boston, his son and his son's wife were killed in a plane crash. He left the university a few days later and never returned. He had always been very private, so no one really knew what happened to him. Some said he went off to raise his granddaughter, others said he just went into hiding to protect his scientific discoveries and mourn his son's death."

"He did all those things," Susan replied.

"Are his papers here?" my mom inquired.

Susan didn't want to answer. My mom turned to me and said, "Tommy, wait here."

My mom grabbed the radio and ran back to the cellar to the open doors. I followed; I couldn't help myself. She leaned over spoke to my dad on the VHF. "Honey, everything is okay, but we are going to stay the night and wait until morning. It's too late to try and get down."

I couldn't hear what my dad said, but I heard my mom reply, "I love you, too. Be back at eight o'clock."

My mom started back up the stairs, with me just ahead of her. When she got to the room, she sat down with Susan. "Susan, it's late. May we stay here with you tonight and then leave in the morning?"

"Can I leave with you?" Susan asked.

"If you want to leave, I will take you. But tonight we can just talk."

The lady cried and hugged my mom. "I would like that. I would like that very much."

The two of them started talking almost nonstop. It was as though I wasn't even there. It seemed my mom had forgotten she came to rescue her son. I didn't care, so long as I didn't have to go back the way I had come, I was happy.

Thirteen

That night in the house, my mom listened as Susan explained everything to her. My mom almost never asked questions, she just listened for several hours. I tried to sleep on the couch but could not stop worrying about snakes getting into the house.

I got up and walked around some time after midnight. My mom was sitting at a desk reading papers by flashlight. Every time I lay back down to try to sleep, I would hear my mom talking to herself. She said things like, "Oh, my god" or "This is unbelievable."

For me, the whole place was so scary that there was no way I was going to fall asleep anyway, so I just stared into space. Rudder was actually snoring.

In the morning, we prepared to exit the house from the cellar. Earlier, my mom had moved Susan's grandfather's body to a more secluded spot so Susan wouldn't have to see him as we walked through.

My mom had Susan gather some personal things. She didn't bring much. The only clothes she had belonged to her grandfather. She looked silly wearing them, but I guessed she had outgrown all of hers. She brought a small doll, some earrings, a watch, and a small knit blanket. That was it.

As we got closer to the door at the cliff, my mom pulled up a small, almost string-size rope. "Mom, don't you think that's a little small to be climbing down on?"

She smiled. "Well, you're right about that. The problem is that when free climbing, one cannot carry much, so I trailed the small cord behind. It is attached to a bigger rope at the bottom of the cliff."

Not long after my dumb observations, my mom had pulled the climbing rope up into the cellar. She then lowered it again to my dad, who attached a bag of pulleys and more rope. She made several passes through the pulleys, and, after rigging up her system, said she was ready.

She reviewed the instructions with Susan several times before clipping her into a harness. She was actually using the seat we used to go to the top of the mast with a halyard called a boson's chair. Surprisingly, Susan seemed relaxed.

My mom called down to my dad, "A surprise is coming first. I'll explain later."

"Roger that," my dad yelled back,

After Susan was all the way down with my dad, my mom put Rudder into a kind of sling and lowered him. Rudder seemed to dig it. Then she looked at me and said, "Okay, Tommy, I'm going now."

I was shocked.

"But, Mom, what about me? How do I get down?"

"Hey, you got up here, find your own way down."

I almost screamed. Before I was sure to lose it, my mom stepped back toward me and said, "Just kidding. I'll lower you down. But take note—Rudder went before you."

I was, for perhaps the first time, speechless. My mom had a way of making you know how much you screwed up without actually saying it. She could even do that to my dad.

Finally, she passed me the harness and lowered me safely to the bottom. During the long drop down the cliff face, I started to change my mind about going down. I knew my father was at the bottom and my arrival was not going to be pretty.

When I touched down, my father didn't say a word. It seemed like the get-out-of-jail-free card was for real. He just kept looking up, waiting for the safe return of my mom. Once she was back, we all headed to the dinghy and then out to the anchored *Imagine*.

Lucky for me, they just ignored me. My parents sat in the cabin with Susan and talked for some time. Caroline was part of the process. Rudder and I hung out on deck, both glad to have avoided another walk through the tunnel.

After about four or five hours, Susan went to Caroline's cabin and closed the door. I was summoned for a family meeting.

My dad began, "We have decided to make Nova Scotia our home for a year."

Caroline, of course, had already known, as she had been in on the conversation all along. I, on the other hand, was taken by surprise. I was not shocked, though, as I had come to learn that my life was in constant change and I had no choice but to go with the flow. It was strange how relaxed I felt about it all.

My mom went on to explain, "The research by Dr. Benson is of global importance. Just the solar-augmented geothermal heating system in that house could save the use of billions of gallons of oil annually.

There are also revolutionary details about many new molecular constructs."

Caroline was looking very excited as she turned to me and said, "Tommy, Mom says the solar energy computer system uses a nano-plasma medium. It even uses analog logic and a carbon-based platform for decision making."

I didn't know how to respond, so I pretended not to hear her. "Tommy, did you hear what I said?" she asked. "There is a functioning analog logic board up there in a nano-plasma construct!"

I ignored her again.

"But, Mom," I asked, "what does that have to do with us?"

My dad replied, "Tommy, Susan has agreed to let your mother and her colleagues from Chicago study her grandfather's papers and the systems in that house. We also need to help her get settled in somewhere. We figure this means staying for about a year."

"But—"

"Tommy," my mom interrupted, "Susan is going to need a lot of help. We want to help her avoid press and public attention. Getting her taken care of is our first priority. My good friend Jenny is a psychologist in Chicago and has agreed to take her in until we get her finances figured out. She needs to be slowly reintroduced into society and Jenny is the perfect person to start the process."

"So where will she get money?" I asked.

"Well, first, we will get her hooked up with an estate attorney to see what might be left behind from her parents and grandfather. Ultimately, though, with just some of the patents on her grandfather's research, she will be entitled to millions."

"Millions?" I repeated.

"Yes," my mom said. "Millions for her, not you."

"But I found her," I replied.

Both my parents looked at me and pretended they hadn't heard that last comment. Caroline asked, "Where will we live?"

"We will rent an apartment near Halifax," my dad said. "You kids can go to regular school, I will get work at the trauma center there, and your mom can work up at the house with her colleagues."

"But what about sailing around the world?"

My dad replied, "Oh, don't worry about that. We are still sailing the globe, just taking a small time-out."

Caroline asked my mom, "What grade will I be in?"

My mom looked at my dad, then at her, and answered, "Well, honey, you have three choices. You can come with me each day and homeschool while we research up at the house. Your second option would be to enter graduate college in Halifax, or, if you want, you can go to regular school and be in seventh grade, but to do that you would have to do your real schoolwork at home."

"I would really like to go to regular school and meet some kids. Would that be okay?"

Mom and Dad said, "Sure."

As usual, she always got what she wanted. "How about me?" I asked.

"How about you what?" my dad said.

"Like with school. What grade and where?"

My dad looked first at my mom, then at me, and said, "I don't know, Tommy. We are looking into reform schools for you."

Caroline laughed. I didn't think it was so funny.

After four months of sailing and covering nearly twenty-four hundred miles, we would stop for the next year. I was faced with the question I had been faced with before: Was this a good thing or bad? I guess I was going to find out. I was a little nervous about going to school in Canada. I didn't even know if they played baseball.

I also wondered if the girls were pretty there. I was hoping they could at least speak English. Or perhaps it would be better if they didn't. Either way, I had survived "the house" and was without snake or bat bites. I was going to start a new school again, and if things were horrible, I knew we would be out of there in less then a year. I was different from a year earlier. With this new little change of plans, I said to myself, "Bring it!"

ABOUT THE AUTHOR

A retired orthopedic surgeon, Dr. Martin is also an accomplished sailor, having covered some fifty thousand ocean miles. He served in the USAF/ANG for seventeen years, leaving with the rank of Major. Dr. Martin is a pilot, a flight surgeon, and a holder of a hundred-ton Masters USCG captain's license.